Droch Fola

The Sumaire Web, Volume 3

Anna Rose

Published by Sumaire Press, 2018.

This is a work of fiction. Similarities to real people, places, or events are entirely coincidental.

DROCH FOLA

First edition. May 10, 2018.

ISBN: 978-1393903017

Written by Anna Rose.

Also by Anna Rose

Tales of the Dragonguard
Aya's Dragon
Sara's Fire

The Sumaire Web
Siofra
Fiach Fola
Droch Fola

Watch for more at www.sumaire.com.

Dedication

As always, I thank my very supportive folks, the splendid K, the inestimable N, the fabulous C, the delightful E, the tenacious T, the Baltimore Raven-loving Mister Moose, and the other special people in my life. I'm the luckiest person in the world, to have you on my side.

Finally, I would like to extend a special Thank You to R, who gave me much-needed information I required about certain aspects of the journey my characters would need to make during the course of this novel. The interwebs are not always the repository of all knowledge, and sometimes you have to step away from the computer and ask someone who's had first-hand experience.

Really.

Author's Note

Writing isn't easy, and don't let anyone try to tell you that it is. The Muse is a whimsical Being, and she's the one who chooses when (and where) to whisper in your ear. More often than not, she's out gallivanting around and nowhere to be found when you need her most. Of course, this also explains those times when I wake from a sound sleep and have to get to my manuscript to start writing whatever has roused me from slumber, before it dissolves away with the dawn and I lose it forever.

Yes, that can and does happen. Dammit.

The best laid plans to have a book out by a specific date are in fact only tentative, try as I might to anticipate my needs beforehand. On top of that, I often seem to live under the delusion that a book is going to be a certain length, only to later discover that it's going to take a whole lot longer to tell the story properly. Rare is the story that "behaves" as you might expect. In most cases, they're like wild things that need to be tamed, but in the process, you're going to have to give them a lot of rope to do it right.

This whole series has been like that. The first novel, "Siofra", was the shortest of them all at a bit more than fifty thousand words. "Fiach Fola" was intended to be perhaps ten to twenty thousand words longer than that, but it ended up at a wee bit over one hundred thousand words. I had thought the book would go a certain way, but other things happened that caused me to adjust my outline a bit and those changes required more research, background and character interplay. Imagine my surprise.

Along those lines, my plan from the start of the series was for it to be a trilogy, and wrote it with that in mind. However, it has become very apparent to me that there is much more to this particular story than originally met the eye. Thus, as of this writing, the final novel is intended to be "Cosán Fola", which is Irish for "Blood Path", bringing this part of Siofra's story to four novels.

A last word about the names of the novels in this series:

As the novels are about Siofra, who *is* an Irish lass at the core of her undead heart, it made sense to have the titles be in her natal language. This will not be the case for all of the planned novels in the Sumaire Web series of novels, so be assured that the tongue twisters will not be constant.

Yes, you read that right. There will be many more novels written about Siofra's universe. They may not be about Siofra or Nathaniel, but there will indeed be more. I hope that is good news for you.

That said, I hope you enjoy reading this latest novel in the series at least as much as I enjoyed writing it.

One

My mind was numb with grief, and I could feel an enormous hole in the center of my being. My oldest friend in the world was no longer a part of my existence, except in my memories of him. The suddenness of his death had even denied me the opportunity to say "goodbye" and for now I was rendered too grief-stricken even to weep.

Janos had been ended after having taken the time to warn me of my own danger. He might have been able to escape if he had taken the opportunity to run instead of contacting me, but he had not, and now he was gone. I could hear Nathaniel saying something to me, but I did not really pay attention. I simply sat on the floor and felt sorry for myself as I stared at the disembodied and oozing head of the lead assassin. Even to me, it felt more than a little ghoulish.

The former lead vampire's eyes were still wide and stared blindly at nothing in particular, showing the massive surprise and disappointment he must have felt at his failure to end me. If Nathaniel had not been able to step in, I would probably now have that same expression on my own face, although wrapped up and on its way to prove my dissolution.

With Nathaniel having completely decapitated my final opponent in our recent battle, there was no chance of him ever coming back to try again. Certainly, with his ending, there remained no opportunity to interrogate him, but sometimes, when you have no other choice; you must go with what is prudent and necessary.

Things had not turned out as the now ended vampire had expected. Generally, when you arrive with superior numbers, things are supposed to go your way. Yes, you might lose a few of your number, but at least one of your small army should be successful in completing the mission.

This was likely intended to have been my own Little Big Horn as far as my enemies were concerned, and they would be mightily disappointed when they discovered they had erred.

One of our opponents had yielded and then fled when given the opportunity, and the other three had been permanently ended. Perhaps they had been young vampires and thus a bit cocky, forgetting in their hubris that the immortality which vampirism offers does have its own wrench to throw into the works. I'd seen such things once or twice in the preceding centuries.

New vampires make excellent cannon fodder in a pitched battle, as they often know so little about their limitations that they are ended before they are able to learn them. Long ago, when a vampire wished to go to war with another, his or her generals would spend some time making new vampires to use as foot soldiers to clear away opposition. If one or more of those new vampires were ended, it was of no great moment. There was always another to take his place. The control that the first feeding blood bond between sire and fledgling created forced the young vampires to obey their orders, even if they would rather have disobeyed.

Those who survived the wars were considered to be seasoned and thus clever enough to merit their continued existence. In some cases with, but a few without, the backing of the Council, I had ended some of those vampires whose luck at survival had resulted in danger to the greater community, so I tended to have strong opinions about the wisdom of vampire conscription. Just because someone has an attribute you desire, it doesn't mean you should go so far as to bring them over. A tiger cub is adorable, but once they mature, they make very poor house pets.

I didn't think my enemies would learn of their failure from the vampire who had fled and thus survived to feed and heal himself. That one would be a fool to believe they'd allow him to exist after having failed in his task. If he was anything resembling smart, he'd be on his way somewhere very far off their map and would lay low until things were safe once more. He'd obviously been smart enough to step away from the battle and go on his own way. That suggested that he was old enough that the blood bond no longer existed between he and his maker. Perhaps that had not been the case with those who had died, but we'd never know that now.

Our attackers had attempted two of the three ways to destroy us, and while they had not been successful in ending us, we hadn't escaped completely unscathed. There was significant damage to my body which would need healing as soon as possible, if I had any intention of retaliating against those who wanted me gone. If they'd simply chosen the third method of destruction, they might actually have been successful, as we'd been tired and abed when they attacked.

The three things that can end a vampire are complete incineration, decapitation or the destruction of enough of the vampire's brain that there's nothing left to animate the body. We're hard to kill, but it's not impossible to make it happen. A bullet of any metallurgic composition is going to end anything if you aim in the right place, and the same can be said of a wooden stake. But no one thinks of putting the stake into the vampire's brain, so those are rarely successful at destroying a vampire. It just pisses them off.

Only a foolish human or fledgling vampire is going to think the conventional wisdom of staking the heart or removing it entirely from the vampire's chest is going to end one of his or her kind. It's a bit of a surprise, the first time someone tries staking you and all it does it hurt enough to make you want to lash out violently. Sometimes it even gives the human doing it enough of a shock that they don't realize their danger until it's too late and they discover they're being held in your arms being sucked dry.

Well, there was that time when I yanked out the stake and stuck it into the human's heart before I realized I needed her to feed on to heal after being wounded in battle. That was one of those experiences when you learn to at least try to think things through before acting.

I will say that I felt in no way sorry for having ended the bitch. She deserved to be ended for having been audacious enough to try to end me. Servants weren't supposed to do things like that. Ever. Her fellow rebels had run away in terror as they saw her die, but I hunted them all and drank them down to heal my wounds.

Most non-French individuals believe that the French Revolution only had to do with the fabled ill-considered words of a French Queen in regard to her starving people, but they would be wrong. The French aristocracy had become so disconnected from the common people that things finally came to a head, revolted and the guillotine subsequently got a hell of a workout. I'd spent quite a lot of time in that country before it all happened, and seeing the way things were mapping out, I knew it was time to find somewhere else to be. Having grown up as someone who had to look out for herself in order to stay safe, I wasn't a fool and knew the danger signs when I saw them.

A little more than half of the Council came to an end during that time, and not a few Havens were razed by rampaging humans. Those humans who had rebelled against their vampire masters and mistresses during those fateful days had met a gruesome end, as none of us who experienced their assault were feeling merciful. That had been the last time the Council stayed in such close proximity to one another if some sort of official meeting was held.

I could hear Nathaniel moving around the room, and the muffled sounds of packing, but I did not really pay attention to it. Instead, I could not help but think about the moment when Janos had been ended, my fertile imagination giving grotesque visuals to the terrible sounds I had heard over the phone. The remembrance of the sounds of his ending were what finally put me over the edge completely.

"Janos is gone, Nathaniel, he's gone!" I couldn't keep my anguish in any longer, as I felt the brimming blood tears tumble over my lower lids and roll down my cheeks, leaving cold trails in their wake. "I heard the instant he ended!"

This couldn't be me. I had never gotten this worked up about losses in the past. Even vampires aren't actually immortal, and would eventually meet their end in one way or another. I'd been acquainted with any number of them who had been ended through their own choice, accident or outright violence, but this ending was different for me. I'd allowed myself to become emotionally connected to Janos and this was the result. This was why I avoided becoming attached to humans whose lives were almost a blink in time compared to my own.

"I know, Siofra, and I'm really sorry about that, but we can't stay here. We have to get the hell out as quickly as possible. I can't imagine they wouldn't be sending reinforcements to be sure we'd been ended. Also, there is no way that the authorities won't be here shortly, since several of those bullets went through the walls," he said to me, shrugging a bulging backpack onto his shoulders, kicking the assassin's head in the general direction of his inert body and then picking me up. "This one is gone, and we have to worry about ourselves now."

Balancing me over one of his broad shoulders in a fireman's carry, Nathaniel exited through the shattered window, holding me in place with one arm while using the other to pull us both up and then onto the roof. I did my best to make it easier for him by using my one good hand to hold onto the worn leather belt that secured his trousers. My damaged arm was not capable of doing anything much beside hang limply, there had been too much muscle damage from my opponents' weapons.

I thought that he would put me down once we reached the roof, but Nathaniel did not even stop to survey the situation. Instead, he leaped from rooftop to rooftop at an easy lope, putting as much distance between us and the massacre as possible. I could hear the distant wail of sirens and knew we'd made our exit none too soon. I wondered what they'd make of the bodies, since they would not appear to be "fresh". While a vampire's body doesn't simply disappear into dust when they are ended in real life, decomposition tends to be a faster kind of affair when our bodies break down into their component parts. If left to its own devices, a vampire's body will be completely gone within a week's time, bones and all.

"It was not a good idea to leave that much evidence behind, Nathaniel. We can't have a coroner looking at any of them too closely," I told him as he sat me down in the shade on an otherwise barren roof about a quarter mile from our former hotel room. "We have to go back to deal with them."

"Don't worry about it, Siofra. I've already taken care of it," he assured me, gesturing back the way we had come. Looking where he pointed, I could see the lazy curl of thick black smoke snaking through the air from the general direction of our former residence. "I grabbed our electronics, money and papers, and then I set fire to a few things before I left the building."

If he'd been able to accomplish all of that while I was wrapped up in my anguish, either he was incredibly fast, or I had been headed down an ugly road mentally. I was glad that he'd shown so much forethought and said so.

"I'm glad you remembered that, Nathaniel. That could have been a serious problem," I said to him, and meant it. "I've had to leave things behind in the past, and once or twice it didn't end well at all."

I was very happy that he had grabbed the electronics. Fire did not always completely destroy the contents of a computer's hard drive, and right now, I could not remember if I had recently deleted my browser's history. Our papers, however, were the most important items he had taken with us. Without them, we'd face a difficult time getting out of the country.

"I left our old papers in the bathroom. Hopefully, they'll survive the flames enough to suggest that we were ended during the course of the fire," he said as he removed the backpack and set it down beside me.

It made a dull thump as it landed beside me, and it dawned on me what kind of weight it carried. "Kind of like what happened in Kabul a few years ago."

Yes, Kabul. Got out of there by the seats of our pants, as far as I was concerned. Remind me to tell you all about that, sometime.

Taking another look at the oily black cloud of rising smoke, it was apparent that he had set fire to quite a few things. We always carried small fire-starter kits with us in the event we were forced to cover our tracks, although we had not had to use them very often. I had discovered them while I was still in the States. They were intended to be used for lighting barbecues and the like, but I had found they worked just as well for doing a significant amount of damage, so I had made sure to keep them on hand.

"Do we have any of those little sticks left over," I asked him. "I don't know when or where we'll be able to pick up more of them."

"Sorry, I had to use all of them and also all of the gel. I was concerned that since there are three bodies in there, I wanted them to be as damaged as possible," he responded. "If things burn well enough, it should also muddy the waters for the assholes who are trying to end us."

"True," I replied. "Once they discover that there are no female remains in there, they might decide to start looking for me with questions in mind."

I was grateful for his foresight and grasped his forearm with my good hand. It still hurt like a son of a bitch, but at least I was able to move it. My other hand, however, hung like a dead fish on the end of a hook.

"I'm glad you were there today, Nathaniel. I don't think I would have made it if I had been on my own," I told him. It was galling to admit that I needed help. I'd always considered myself to be self-sufficient, as well as ready and able to meet any challenge, but this time, that hadn't been true. "I'm damned lucky to have you with me."

He would not meet my eyes, but squeezed my hand with his own before gently breaking free. Even without our old newborn fledgling's emotional connection, I could feel his discomfort. I wanted to ask him about it, but he did not give me the chance.

"I'm going to go get you something to eat so you can heal up. We can't stay here very long," he said thickly, then disappeared down the other side of the building. I heard the faint sound of his feet hitting the ground, and then nothing but the sounds of the surrounding community. Since I could not really move very well until I fed successfully, I closed my eyes and let the aromas and cacophony of the area lull me into an almost hypnotic state.

I fell into a dreamlike state filled with the memories gained during my centuries of knowing Janos. What had seemed like an eternity now felt almost fleeting, and it twisted at my heart as a spinning wheel twists yarn.

Our first meeting had been when we were selected to end a particularly rebellious vampire. He had not much liked me when we met, nor me, him. He saw me as some uncivilized Irish yokel, and I had seen him as a pampered member of the aristocracy who'd been given a gift he did not deserve.

We'd spent eight months together during that hunt, learning that each of us was very wrong about the other. Along the way, he taught me many things that would enable me to survive as long as I have. I had indeed been cocky when I met him, and he showed me that I was an insufferable little shit in rather ungentle ways.

There was the day he decided that he was comfortable enough with me to introduce me to his wife, Estelle. Within a few moments of our introduction, she had enfolded me in a ladylike bear hug, if such a thing could exist, and told me to think of her as family. The rush of feeling I'd experienced from her welcome was something I had no experienced in over a century.

Janos' wife was close to my height, but just slightly taller than I. However tall she was, when Janos held her in his arms, she only had to left her face a little to kiss his full lips. When he held me, however, he would rest his chin atop my head and enfold me in his arms in a protective and fatherly way.

Estelle had a small overbite and perfect little teeth that shone with the play of light across them. When she'd been brought over, she had dark blonde mid-length curly hair, that when she allowed it to hang loose, hung to midback, and because of the peculiarities of what we were, that had never changed. Estelle normally wore it pulled up in a neat bun atop her head, but when she wore it down, Janos could often be found with the fingers of one hand loosely tangled in it while the other would play with Estelle's dainty fingertips.

I thought about how he'd never be able to do that again and I mourned that loss as well.

Then I recalled the innumerable games we'd played over the centuries: anything from games that lasted a half hour, to some that lasted more than fifty years. I wondered what had happened to the delicately carved ebony and alabaster chessboard I had given him on the hundredth anniversary of our first meeting, and which he had kept in his office. We'd started our latest chess marathon game about five years ago.

His sense of humor and his warm laugh. He had had an arsenal of dirty jokes that only proved that some off-color humor had been around since at least the Renaissance. I had never dared to ask him from whom he had learned some of them, as I did not want him to think I doubted their origins.

His deep voice that could make me feel at home, or send shivers up my spine. He would have made a fantastic radio announcer, if he had not been so cautious about staying off human radar. His voice could slide so easily from laughter into something very serious or even dangerous, and that could happen in the space of mere seconds.

These were things I would never again experience or share with him, and it hurt me more than anything in my life ever had before. Excluding my maker, Andreas, with whom I had very little to do, Janos had been the longest acquaintance of my existence.

I came back to myself to find Nathaniel touching my shoulder gently. Opening my eyes, I saw an unconscious human on the ground in front of me. I hadn't been breathing, so the scent of human hadn't caught my attention until the human was right in front of me.

There was a large goose-egg on the human's head, but I saw no blood, so Nathaniel had been very careful while capturing this human. I could see from looking at Nathaniel's face that he had already fed, which had been the smart thing to do. Who knew when we'd have the opportunity to feed again?

"There were two of them, so I fed from the one and brought this one back for you," he told me, gesturing at the oblivious lump of flesh on the ground before me. "Feed and then we can find a safer place to hole up."

With a little initial help from Nathaniel, who held the human up for me, I opened up the human's throat and drank deeply. As feeling and mobility returned to the damaged portions of my body, I pulled the human close and drank as much as I could before I heard his heartbeat begin to flutter. He never awoke, which was fine with me, since I had no desire to have a wrestling match at the moment.

I felt my flesh repairing itself and heard the soft slither of skin and muscle as they flowed over themselves in the course of healing. Feeling returned to my lower body as the parched tissues soaked up the blood that filled them up. Pain disappeared, leaving behind only a feeling of sticky well-being.

Soon, except for the blood and gore that marked my clothing, there would be no outward sign of the battle that I had only barely managed to survive. I'd lost track of how many times I'd been in a similar situation, damage-wise, and was once again thankful that vampires don't heal human-slow.

I pushed the body off of my lap and stood, the human's blood not really making that much of a noticeable stain on my clothing. I already had too much of my own fluids all over them. I wondered aloud how I was going to be able to get from one place to another without getting too much attention.

"I tried to find something appropriate, but it was a choice between feeding and clothing, and feeding's much more important," he replied. "We may have to stay here until the sun goes down before we move out."

I was not very happy about that, as opportunistic flies had already begun to settle on the corpse and start laying their eggs. Nature's clean-up squad never misses a chance to create a new generation of janitors. While I understood their importance in the scheme of things, it did not mean that I liked being around them.

Since we were going to have to remain on the roof for at least another few hours, I carefully moved the body to the opposite side of the roof. I was pleased that the corpse's clothing, although fouled when its sphincters released upon the human's death, kept the worst of the filth contained.

"At least it's not getting as hot now during the day, but that thing's still going to get ripe in the heat of the day," Nathaniel opined, to which I nodded. "I'm sorry."

I laughed, but he did not join in. Nathaniel was rarely out of good humor, so his reticence concerned me. Hopefully he would be willing to talk about it.

"There isn't anything you need to be sorry about. I'm just glad we survived," I reassured him. "Are you okay?"

He looked at me and I could see the blood tears brimming in his eyes, his lower lip trembling a bit. It was like looking at a child trying so very hard to not allow tears to come.

"You may not like what I'm going to say, Siofra, but I have to say it," he said to me.

"What is it, Nathaniel?"

"I know you're upset about Janos being ended, but I didn't really know him," he confessed, wringing his hands together. It was as though he had once again reverted to being a little boy and appeared to feel guilty and embarrassed at his discomfort. "I came so close to losing you this morning."

"But they were not successful. We're both still here," I tried to ease his distress. "We've survived to see another day, against nasty odds."

"Siofra, I don't know what I would do if I lost you," he said softly. "You're the only family I have now."

It hit me like a shot and I cursed myself for being a worthless shit. It had been there right in front of me, and I'd either not seen or simply refused to see it.

I had been feeling so sorry for myself, feeling that I had lost my family, and had forgotten that I had a family of my own. Now I felt guilty and at least as terrible as he appeared to feel. When I had been turned, I had thought my entire family dead and gone, unlike Nathaniel, who had a couple sisters and a father he had to leave behind when he became a vampire. He had left them to ensure their safety, but that did not ease the pain of the wound that permanent separation caused.

I had created my own family when I had made the choice to turn him all those years ago, and I was being a real asshole now. It did not matter how upset I was, my first thought should have been for Nathaniel, but I had been selfish. Still hating myself and wondering how I could ever fully apologize for my idiocy, I moved close to him, taking his face between my hands and staring deep into his eyes.

"I'm sorry, Nathaniel. I was all caught up in my own thoughts, and forgot to think about how this affected you. The only reason you and I survived this is because we were together and were able to fight them off. Barely." I told him. "I know I wouldn't have made it without you at my side."

His tears broke through the dam of his eyelids and ran down his face, unheeded. I reached up and wiped his tears away with my thumbs, smearing his cheeks with a thin layer of blood-colored fluid in the process, making it appear as though he wore blush.

Funny how blood tears retain their real blood color when the blood we ingest normally becomes so very dark. Maybe someday I'll take the time to ask someone why, but that was not important right now. Nathaniel was the important thing right now. Hell, Nathaniel would always only be the only important thing.

He's my family. The only "real" family I have, when it comes right down to it. Do I make a "blood relative" comment here or not?

Probably should not.

"We both survived, Nathaniel. That's what's important here," I told him. "Now we have to find whoever ended Janos and then tried to end us. They're not going to stop until we force the issue."

"I don't want to see you ended, Siofra," he replied. "Isn't there any other way to deal with this?"

"No, they're going to keep coming after us until they succeed, unless we end them, first. As for my being ended, it's always a possibility, Nathaniel, but I'm going to try my damndest to keep that from happening. Let's get off this roof as soon as possible and get the hell out of this country!"

Two

While we waited for the shadows of nightfall to arrive, Nathaniel and I brainstormed our exit from Iraq.

Using the airport was out of the question. I knew that from the start, and it did not take me long to explain why to Nathaniel.

They would be looking for us, well, me, really, and the airport was the most logical place for them to post their spies. Instead, we'd have to use alternative transportation, and right now, that was looking like we'd have to take the long way, heading northwest and up into Jordan. Yes, you heard that right. Jordan. That country had reasonably friendly relations with Western Europe, so it would be less of a hassle flying from there to Germany or England. The same could not be said of flying between Iraq and either of those counties.

Most of that trip would be through sparsely populated, but nevertheless, very dangerous territory. However, that would still be better than trying to fly out and being ended along with an entire plane full of humans. It would not surprise me if our enemies would take things that far, as I had seen the Council do it to eliminate vampires who were trying to flee their brand of "justice".

With a little luck, it would not take too long to travel the few hundred miles between our location in the Al-Anbar Province and the border. I did not want to involve anyone we might know here, as they would be a potential target for our pursuers. If they did not know about them yet, they certainly did not need to know about them now.

As it was, the Leone we knew were in the mountainous Northeastern part of the country, and we would be headed northwest, so there was only a small chance we'd even encounter strange Leone on our journey, which suited me just fine.

Looking at our belongings, I saw that we had just about everything we needed for the moment. The laptops were nestled in the heavily padded backpack we'd purchased in Baghdad only a few weeks earlier, and as long as we were able to get a set of clean clothing for each of us, we'd be set. We were both a bloody mess after having fed, so the clothing we wore now would not cut it in public.

As the sun began its tapdance on the horizon, we were finally able to descend from our perch on that anonymous roof. We'd spent our time discussing our escape and watching the residence hotel in which we'd been staying burn to the ground. Both Nathaniel and I could smell the scent of charred flesh that indicated human bodies had burned in the fire. No, I did not feel bad about it. We had made good our exit, and for now, that was all that mattered.

While Nathaniel ran off to find appropriate clothing for himself, I found a handy clothesline and filched a pair of pants and a shirt that was near enough my size that they would be useful. Dressing in western-style men's clothing made more sense at the moment, as women would be much more closely looked at.

While I had been out "clothes shopping" for myself, I located and then pocketed an unattended cellphone that I found on a windowsill off a little side street. Moving some distance away from where I had found it, I used it to contact someone I knew who lived in London. I knew they could be trusted, so I let them know what was going on, and where we would be within the next few days, if all went as planned.

When I finished the call, I deleted the number I had dialed from the phone's memory, removed the SIMM card, and then threw the cheap phone onto the ground hard enough to shatter it. There was no reason to carry it around with me, as I could always get another the same way I had gotten its predecessor. I used one of my knives to cut the SIMM into several tiny pieces and then tossed the plastic and foil confetti into any number of trash receptacles along my path.

Perhaps that was overkill, but I was not comfortable until I had done so. There were too many people who were probably out there looking for us, and it was not worth random discovery.

Pulling one of my boot knives from its sheath, I grabbed my hair and hacked it off at the nape of my neck. It would return in all its glory when next I fed. As I nearly always did after cutting my hair, I held it and watched as the severed hair first turned a limp and sickly white, then crumbled to dust in my hand. It never seemed to survive being parted from my body.

Vampires don't lose mass permanently, even if we lose a limb in the course of feeding or fighting. Provided a vampire drinks enough blood, we can regenerate even our entire lower body if necessary. Gruesome to behold, but in a grotesquely fascinating way. Regrowing my waist-length hair would only take about a quarter of a pint of blood, at most, to accomplish. I had done this before during our time in Iraq, but it always bothered Nathaniel when I did so.

He seemed to have a thing for my long, red hair. Maybe it's a guy thing. I don't really know. Over the years, there had been many a time when he had pulled out the comb from his pocket and spent hours just gently combing through my hair, carefully removing the knots and leaving it perfectly groomed by the time he had finished.

One night, he had found a single gray strand in the mass of hair on my head, and had pulled it out. Of course, the next time I fed, it had come back, and he had assumed a pouty expression at that particular quirk of what we were. Fortunately, the hair was buried under a heavy layer of deep red hair, so he and I were probably the only ones who even knew about it.

I heard Nathaniel's gasp and turned to face him. He was clad in a badly-fitted *thawb* but it appeared that he had not gotten a *keffiyeh* scarf to finish it all off. I did not ask him where he had gotten the clothing, I was just glad he had been able to find something quickly so that we could be on our way.

"You cut your hair," he said in an almost accusatory tone. "I hate it when you do that."

"They're going to be looking for a woman with long red hair, even if I braid it to pull it up. They may not realize that I'd cut it and try to pass as male. You know perfectly well that it's going to grow back as soon as I feed again, so don't worry about it," I reassured him. "You men and your long hair fetishes!"

"I like the way it looks on you, Siofra," he replied. "When you leave it down, it sometimes moves forward to cover your face a little bit, and it makes you look feral."

Feral. Hmm, that sounded intriguing. We'd have to discuss that at some future time when we were not running for our lives. I smiled at him and then chuckled.

"Well, you'll get your 'feral' Siofra back soon enough, Nathaniel," I said, grinning. "We need to get ourselves some wheels that include at least a full tank of fuel and get moving!"

After pulling the missing *keffiyeh* from seemingly nowhere and arranging it on his head, he now looked the part of a local, unless you looked closely enough. Glancing at me, he seemed to understand my question.

"Not my favorite thing to wear, so why put it on any sooner than absolutely necessary?" With that, he gave me a saucy wink and a sketchy bow, then darted away on his appointed errand, his *keffiyeh* making slapping noises in the wind as he left. Not quite Lawrence, but he would do.

Wheels ended up being a beat up old Japanese pickup truck that was missing its bed. Rusted out, it was probably barely holding together, but if it could get us where we needed to go, I was all for it. Fortunately, it had a manual transmission, so it was easy to push it out to where its starting should go fairly unnoticed alongside the noises of the night.

The truck started with an asthmatic wheeze, chugging a bit before settling into the familiar rhythm of an internal combustion engine. There was a slight hiccup every so often, but not so much as to cause me much concern. What did cause me some concern was the hole in the floor that allowed me to see more of the terrain we would cross than I cared to survey.

"Well, this is probably the best ride we could get for now," I conceded to Nathaniel. "Did you know that I can see scorpions on the ground underneath us right now?"

"For now, it has fuel and can move under its own power," he replied softly. "If you see anything trying to crawl it, either step on it or hit it in the head."

"Oh, that's reassuring," I sniped at him, which made him laugh.

"The important thing for now is just getting the hell out of here," he said. "Pretty would just have attracted more attention, and you know that."

Yes, I did know that, and nodded wordlessly.

"For whatever reason, it was parked away from busy human traffic areas, so it made sense to take it," he said. "Plus, the human left the keys in the sun visor. You'd think he was asking to have it stolen."

"Probably not. It's a common place for people to put keys when it's a shared vehicle. It was more frequent in the 1960's in the western United States, but then, the hippies were a fairly trusting group of people," I told him. I remembered more than a few tasty meals during that time, usually from humans who had only just begun to drop out, tune in and turn on, or whatever it was they said then. The drugs had not yet begun to poison their bodies and their blood. "Keep in mind, though, that it's only a matter of time before it's discovered to be missing, so we've got to scat."

Our well-rusted chariot currently held about three quarters of a tank of fuel, so with luck, it could get us close to where we needed to go. We'd have to hoof it from there, if we were not fortunate enough to either find fuel or another vehicle. I would prefer a vehicle, as coming in to the border on foot would cause more questions and investigation than either of us desired.

We watched the city lights recede through the dirt rainbow of our rear window. I kept expecting someone to notice us and know we did not belong to the truck, but Lady Luck was with us and we left unmolested. Even so, I did not relax until the last light faded into the blackness behind us. As we had excellent night vision, we drove with the headlights off. There was no sense in drawing more attention to ourselves than was absolutely necessary.

For now, Nathaniel drove. I wanted the chance to sit back for a bit and just rest and think. He did not try to engage me in conversation. He had long ago learned that when I was like this, it was best to leave me alone. Yes, there were often times when we'd pass long hours of travel discussing everything from our most recent feeding to politics to sports, but for now, this was not one of those times.

I don't know how much time had gone by before he interrupted my dozy thoughts.

"I'm starting to pick up the scent of humans, Siofra," he said over the thrum of the truck's motor. "Can you smell them, too?"

Since vampires have no need to breathe, I had not been sampling the air, but allowed myself to do so now. Yes, there it was: the stench of unwashed bodies, coupled with the rank odor of new death. My natural curiosity was piqued.

"Whoever it is, they either haven't seen a tub of bathwater in a long time, or they've been somewhere pretty hot," I opined. "The weather's been cooling lately, so I'm not sure which it is, though."

"It wouldn't hurt to get in another feeding while we have the opportunity," Nathaniel suggested hopefully. I could see his eagerness at the thought of a hunt shining in his eyes. The part of my offspring I thought of as "Bloodthirsty Nathaniel" was clearly present tonight. "Who knows when that will happen again?"

Damn it, he was right. I would have preferred to keep going, but filling ourselves to satiation was our best course of action. It might be a bit uncomfortable at first, as our bodies distributed the excess blood to less hydrated parts but beggars can't be choosers, can they?

"See if you can find somewhere to park this thing and we'll hunt them on foot," I told him. "And for god's sake, take the keys with you! This isn't Ride-Share, you know."

He chuckled darkly and put the truck into neutral before turning off the engine and allowing it to roll for several hundred feet under its own power before coming to rest beside some boulders along the side of the road. We slipped out, Nathaniel gently closing the door until the latch *clicked*, and then moved out to find our next meal. There was no sense in making any more noise than was absolutely necessary.

Sniffing the air, I judged the humans to be about a quarter mile from our location. I nodded to Nathaniel and he moved out in a wide arc in order to circle around behind them. We'd only scented two or three humans, so there was every chance we could take them all and make a feast of them.

My hair was still chopped short, so I was not immediately identifiable as a female. I should be able to get fairly close to them before they realized I was not merely a short-statured male, but once they saw my bright red hair, they would instantly know that I was not a local. That did not bode well for anyone here, male or female, as this area was noted for insurgent activity, and had been for several decades.

I moved quickly toward their encampment, for that's what it was, hidden in the middle of a cluster of rocks. They had no fire, which meant that I would be able to see them long before they saw me, which was always an advantage when you're a vampire on the hunt. It would be even better if I could take them out, one by one. Already my hunger was piqued at the thought of feeding to the point where I could swallow no more. I had not had that opportunity in a very long time now.

As I got closer, I heard the voices of three male humans. They seemed to be discussing some meeting that had either already happened or would be happening soon. I did not really care. All I wanted was their lifeblood. Their human bullshit meant nothing to me.

I waited until one of them moved off to relieve himself a short distance away. He was a small man, not much taller than I, so he should not be too difficult to subdue. I followed along behind him on cat feet, stepping as he did and not making a sound. I waited as he moved his robes aside and pulled out his dick to piss before I struck.

He was too involved in making lazy circles of urine on the ground to notice me before it was too late. I moved in and clamped one hand over his mouth, while moving close enough to rip a hole in the side of his throat.

His blood fountained, out, bathing me in its hot crimson river as I locked my lips on the hole and began to suck his life down into my own body. The hole I had created was really too big, and I knew I would have to work fast to get as much of his blood into me before his body died and made what remained undrinkable to me. The human batted feebly at me, his strength deserting him as I devoured the precious fluid that had kept his heart beating and his brain operating.

I let go as I felt his body begin to die, and I dropped him on the ground, to finish the process. The local insects and predators could have what was left. He was of no further use to me. I could see his eyes staring blindly and beginning to dull as what was left of his life-energy departed and left behind a corpse that cooled quickly in the early spring night air.

I returned to the camp as I heard a commotion arise and saw Nathaniel, one hand clamped around one of the remaining humans' arms and fighting off his compatriot, who was attempting to defend himself with a long knife of some sort. A knife. How prosaic.

At this point, I had so much blood in me that my skin felt stretched and was almost painful, but I knew that this would only be a temporary situation until whatever pressure balance was achieved within me and the blood I had consumed was evenly distributed throughout my flesh. My hair, as expected, had regrown with the ingestion of new blood, and now danced around the small of my back, as lush and red as it had ever been. This was definitely one of the perks of being a vampire. I had regrown entire limbs in the past, but it was a far more gruesome process than my hair simply returning to its original length.

Wondering whether or not I should step in to intercede on Nathaniel's behalf, a quick look at his face let me know that he was enjoying himself. Of course, he had always been at home with more challenging hunts, so this did not really surprise me in the least. I decided I would only step in if he indicated he wanted me to do so. Once upon a time, I had worried that he was taking on more than he could handle, but eventually I had learned that he was far more capable than I had realized.

The human he had grabbed by one arm had already fainted from sheer fright, so now Nathaniel let him dangle on the ground as he easily deflected the other human's attempts to stab and slice him with his knife. I knew that his true target was the human he now fought. The feeding that resulted from that victory would give him far more satisfaction than one taken from the one who was currently unconscious and drooling all over himself, but the human would not know that. He was obviously trying to defend the other human, not knowing that he stood a better chance of surviving if he simply high-tailed it out of there.

Well, not really a better chance, as we'd still hunt him down and eat him, but certainly better than fighting to the point of exhaustion and then being unable to defend himself any further. Why tell him, though? It was much more fun for Nathaniel this way.

The point came, however, when the human managed to slice Nathaniel's forearm, and instead of blood oozing from the wound, dark thick fluid emerged. The human, his whoop of triumph changing to a grunt of astonishment and fear, stumbled and fell to one knee. I could suddenly smell the pungent stink of his fear as he realized he'd bitten off far more than he could chew, and now he was choking in it.

He blurted out a string of words that were too garbled for me to understand, dropping the knife and holding his arms wide in a gesture of surrender. Maybe he thought that by doing so, he would save his own life.

The human could not have been more wrong.

Nathaniel hissed at him, dropping the unconscious human almost absently and instead descending upon the one who had spent the past fifteen minutes worrying at him. Nathaniel's fangs were now evident, and I smelled the sharp tang of urine as the terrorized and terrified human soiled himself.

Although he tried to run away, the human was unable to find his feet and instead fell backward into the dust as Nathaniel advanced. He scrambled to grab up the knife again, and it was almost comical to see him glance at the knife in his hand, and then at six feet of angry vampire descending upon him. I saw the moment he realized that he would not stand a chance against the monster he faced, and saw despair finally emerge in his expression.

I had kept to the shadows, but decided it was time to step forward. Not wanting the unconscious human to rouse and take advantage of his freedom, I moved to him and rolled him over on his stomach pulling his arms behind him and strapping them and his feet together with lengths of cloth torn from the bottom of his *thawb*. One more strip of cloth would serve as a gag to keep him from yelling for help or just being verbally obnoxious.

It would not hurt to take something with us for a snack later on, if we needed it. To be perfectly honest, we probably would need one, as there was little chance we'd make it across the desert in perfect shape. There were just too many possibilities for human mischief between here and Iraq's single border with Jordan.

An anguished scream pierced the night, and I looked over to see that Nathaniel now had the human bent over backward, and was standing over him while drinking slowly from smallish puncture wounds he had created on the human's throat. There was a kind of deliberate cruelty to his actions, which probably had to do with the flesh wound the human had given him. He tended to react badly when his prey fought back hard enough to damage him. The wound in question was now a thing of the past, with nothing remaining to even suggest its former presence.

That it had healed over did not matter to Nathaniel. He was caught up in the excitement of feeding, and almost nothing would distract him from that. With the wounds he had made in the human's throat, very little blood was wasted, unlike my own recent feeding.

The human continued to scream for a very long time, although near the end, his scream became thin and weak before it finally faded away. There was no one to help him from miles around, but perhaps he had entertained the remotest hope that someone would have come to his rescue.

Now the human was just an inert meat bag that would spoil quickly in the harsh desert.

Nathaniel had come a very long way from the fledgling who had been so shocked at what he had done, after his first kill. The change in thinking that eventually comes in the first few months after one is turned had been true for him as well. Perhaps it's a mental self-defense mechanism that operates to keep the vampire sane, since one goes from being human to being something that preys on humans in order to survive. Whatever it might be, Nathaniel was an accomplished hunter, and beyond a physical resemblance to a long-dead human called Nathaniel Ian Bock, they were no longer the same individual.

"Well, you made a hell of a mess of yourself," he commented as he looked at me. "Any particular reason you felt a need to spill half of him onto the sand?"

"I let the enjoyment of it all get the best of me. You know what that's like, and you also know that I normally hate losing any of it," I replied. "I fed pretty well earlier today, so things were not desperate. It was okay to play a bit."

"Playing's cool, but now you look like you've been seriously abused, and we don't have any spare clothes for you," Nathaniel noted, eyeing me up and down. "You're stuck like that until we can either find you new ones, or you find a way to wash them."

Bursting into laughter, I gestured at the hogtied but still unconscious human on the ground. A handy warm blood bag, waiting to be emptied, and it was ours.

"Let's take that one with us, we can both feed on him later," I told him, using the clean sand from the ground to scrub away some of the clotted blood on my shirt. "We may not have a bed on that thing, but there's room enough on the floorboards for him to lie until we decide that his part of the trip is over."

Nathaniel picked the human up and slung him over his shoulder and we returned to the pickup. The human only regained consciousness as we wedged his body into the truck, and it happened quickly and with a bit of noise on his part. Fortunately, the gag we'd jury-rigged together did a good job at keeping most of his utterances contained. I had no desire to hear anything he would have to say, anyway.

Apparently, it turned out that it would be a tighter fit for the human on the floorboards of the truck, but I did not really care about his comfort, so it was not really a big deal for me. All I cared about was that he would still be alive when the time came to feed from him, so as long as he could breathe and was not having holes poked in him, I did not give a shit about him.

"We're going to have to try to either find some fuel, or another set of wheels, Siofra. We've only got about a quarter tank of gas left, which should get us another hundred miles or so before we're out of luck," Nathaniel told me as he turned the ignition and looked at the gauges in front of him as they came back to life once again. "In the event we can't find it, we'll have to deal with the human sooner, rather than later."

I was glad that Nathaniel was speaking English right now, because I did not want to have him start thrashing around on the floor. For most of the people in the area, if they spoke a second language, it was French, rather than English. While I felt the human tense during our conversation, I did not sense the panic that our words would have caused if he had understood them.

How would you feel if you heard yourself being referred to as "the human"? It probably wouldn't make you feel very good, I would wager. I had had a few situations where my prey had overheard my plans for them, and the results generally were unpleasant on both sides of the predator/prey relationship.

The majority of our conversation concerned our plans for after we got to Europe and began our hunt for the people who had ended Janos.

A little over an hour's drive later, the fuel gauge was just short of hitting the danger zone, and we were making a far more concerted effort to find some source of fuel for our four-wheeled rust bucket. We'd passed a few former petrol stations during that time, but they were either abandoned, or completely out of fuel, with no idea of when the fuel storage tanks would be filled once more. Along the way, I grabbed a few gas cans that contained at least some amount of fuel and put the result into the tank, in the hopes of extending our drive as much as possible.

As you may well imagine, the gas cans had not been easy to locate. Nathaniel had stopped outside of the various villages while I went out and started my scavenger hunt for fuel. It was event difficult to find empty cans, they were apparently so valuable to their owners. Eventually, I was forced to enter their homes to make a wider search. That proved to be my best idea, as ultimately, I found that most humans were hiding their gas cans in their homes. I restrained myself from snacking, as I did not want to raise any more suspicions than were absolutely necessary. Tonight, they were losing gasoline, not their lives. They might not see the difference when they awakened and discovered its loss, but that's the way the world seems to operate, in my experience.

Due to our frequent stops in search of fuel, we only managed to cover a little more than a few hundred miles by the time the sun began its crawl up from the horizon. It was five hundred miles, more or less, from our original location to our destination in Jordan, so we still had quite a ways to go.

The roads were not fantastic, so we could not travel at Autobahn-type speeds, and ended up mostly traveling at about 70 miles per hour. We needed to find either more fuel or another vehicle, soon, with a different vehicle being preferable. Who knew what kind of kerfuffle had arisen out of our theft of the one we now used, and if anyone was on the lookout for us as a result.

Our human passenger started moaning again, irritating me out of my thoughts, so I kicked him hard enough to make him stop. The human glared at me, mumbling something through his gag, and wiggled a bit more. I knew a threat when I saw one, and finally reached down to choke him once again into unconsciousness.

"We're going to have to deal with him soon," Nathaniel said to me. "You can't keep kicking him and choking him whenever he becomes inconvenient. Either we eat him or we end him, but we can't drag this out. I'm not hungry in the least, so I lean toward the former, unless you're feeling peckish now."

"You're right," I replied. "When we encountered the three of them I thought it was a good idea to put one aside for later, but realistically, it isn't necessary."

"What do you want to do with him? Let him loose or end him?"

"I'm not sure what he's seen, so we'll have to end him," I decided. "He could have been playing 'possum while you fed, and we don't need the area lit up with reported monster sightings."

Nathaniel laughed and slapped me on the shoulder before returning his attention to the road.

"We should get rid of him before the sun comes up any further and especially before we get to a city, Nathaniel. Easier to hide him out in this area than where there'll be more humans around," I suggested. He grunted his agreement and pulled to the side of the road. We waited until a small pack of vehicles passed before I got out and began to pull the soon-to-be corpse out of the truck. No sense garnering any more attention than we must.

This time, I stayed with the truck, and Nathaniel took the human for disposal. Waiting until we could see no traffic in either direction, Nathaniel swung the human over this shoulder and then jogged into the brush until I could no longer see him, even with my enhanced vision. I waited a good half hour before he returned and dropped the now unnecessary cloth restraints into my hand with a grin.

"In the condition he's in, I don't think we'll have to worry about keeping him tied up. It seemed thrifty to hold onto these, however," he said, smiling. "You up to driving?"

"Sure," I said, putting the rags into a back pocket and then climbing into the driver's seat. "It's your turn to doze."

"Thanks, Siofra," he said. "I need it."

He closed his eyes, putting his long legs up on the console and folding his arms behind his head as a makeshift pillow. I always enjoyed watching him relax, and this was no exception. I let him rest for about an hour, when I could wait no longer.

"We need to find a place to hole up for the day. Maybe we can find another vehicle while we're here. I've still got the medallion, so I'll pull another rock off it to see if we can find one more easily. At least one with a full tank of gas," I said, breaking our long silence. "Right now, we'll be fortunate to get another fifty miles out of this tank."

Nathaniel opened his eyes and glanced over at the fuel gauge, then straightened up in his seat. He gave a monstrous stretch, and I heard the crackle of his joints as they slid back into place. Yes, even with vampires, a good stretch will often do you good.

"It looks like the day's just about officially begun," he noted. "We can stop in the nearest town and get a wash-up and maybe some fresh clothing, if we're lucky."

And so, some forty miles later, we found ourselves entering Ar Rutbah, a city some one hundred miles or so from the Iraqi-Jordanian border. Nathaniel had taken over driving, as the locals would very likely look askance at a woman driving, and he talked his way past the sentries who guarded the city that resided on a high plateau. He was respectful, friendly and slipped each one a semi-precious stone from off the medallion I still wore concealed around my neck. With those hard credentials duly approved, we were allowed to pass.

One of the guards had directed Nathaniel to his own home, along with whatever formula should be said to gain entrance in order to get a bath and even changes of clothing. He had looked me up and down, and then said that he had a son who was my size, and that for consideration, I could wear something from that collection.

"He has to know I'm female," I said to Nathaniel as we continued on our way. "Why would he suggest his son's clothing? I get nervous when humans start being helpful."

"I think he's a friendly," Nathaniel suggested. "He knows perfectly well that we're not from here and that we're just trying to get the hell out of Dodge, and so he's being helpful. That, and I gave him one of those gold knobs from the medallion."

The medallion in question was designed specifically to be a way to easily carry funds, and so its gems were set in such a way as to be easily removed with slightly greater than normal pressure. It also possessed knobs around its rim that could be removed and used in a pinch to grease palms. In this case, it had bought us baths and clothing, so I was not going to complain very loudly. Shortly, I would have access to my regular funds, and we would no longer need to rely on the uncertainty provided by a chunk of metal and jewels in order to get by.

The guard's home was on the opposite side of town. It was unprepossessing, but if it included the ability have a hot bath or shower, I was all for it. A young boy of about thirteen answered the door, and from looking at him, I could see he was the one the guard was thinking of when he was considering what clothing he might have available for me to wear.

With the utterance of a very familiar sound used by a nighttime cartoon character, we were quickly ushered into the guard's home and I was shown to the bathroom. The boy seemed delighted and even amused at having heard Nathaniel's password, and so the child began peppering him with questions about the show. When Nathaniel expressed surprise that the boy even knew anything about the program, the child explained that it still aired, and was still quite popular.

After Nathaniel and I had both showered and changed into clean clothing, the boy, who had identified himself to us as "Rami", attempted to press us with food. We politely declined his offer, indicating that we were still full from our last meal, as indeed we were.

"How can you not be hungry after so long a drive," he wanted to know, reasonably.

"We are on a fast, and so cannot eat until nightfall," I explained to him, after finding out Rami had no compunctions about speaking with strange females. "We will have our dinner once the sun is down again."

"We are looking for a different vehicle," Nathaniel said to him. "Would you know of anyone who is looking to sell one that will have enough fuel to get us at least another three hundred miles?"

Rami pursed his lips and thought for a long time, then shook his head.

"There was a car a few houses down that was for sale a few days ago, but I think it has gotten a buyer already," he confessed. "If you wait until morning, I can ask around for you."

"Maybe we can go speak to the seller and see if he knows of another vehicle for sale, then," Nathaniel suggested, getting up from the chair in which he had been resting. "It is important that we keep going, if we are to stay on schedule."

Reluctantly, the boy took Nathaniel out the door and off to the neighbor's place. I puttered around and looked at the morning paper. On one of the inner pages, there was an article about a massive hotel fire Ramadi, and it appeared as though there were several unfortunate deaths because of it, including a foreign man and woman who had been staying there. The article indicated they were still looking for their bodies, but it was believed they had been incinerated, due to the extreme heat of the blaze, the cause of which was still being investigated.

So, at least for now, we were considered to be ended, which should give us some wiggle room to get out of the country and into a safer place. I was folding the paper back into its original shape and putting it back when the door opened, and the boy and Nathaniel returned. The boy was shaking his head, while Nathaniel's face bore a wide grin.

"Well, the seller had indeed sold the car the other day, but it turned out that he had another car that he was willing to part with for two of the nicer rocks we had. It's got a full tank of fuel, as well as two full gas cans to take along with us, in the event we end up needing them. This one is one of those little cars like you see in Europe, but if it will get us to the border..." he let his voice trail off.

"Wonderful!" I exulted. "Let's get a move-on, then. We have no time to waste. I saw an article about what happened yesterday, but it's only going to hold them off for so long before they get suspicious."

"Oh? I'm surprised they covered it," he said slowly.

"Who knows why? Maybe the ones who are after us pressed for information and this is what happened as a result. Whatever the reason, it was not brushed under the carpet," I replied. "We don't want anyone putting two and two together and getting four instead of five."

He laughed.

"You really like saying that, don't you?" he chuckled. He was right. I had said it more than once over the years.

"I read it somewhere and I guess it stuck with me," I told him. "So sue me."

He laughed harder and started for the door, pressing a rather nice shiny rock into the hand of the boy who had been our host when the boy reached out to shake his hand in parting.

"Thank you very much for your hospitality, young man," Nathaniel told him. "This extra here is for you. You may either give it to your father, or you may set it aside for when you further your education or start your own household."

The boy looked at the two carat stone that wobbled in the palm of his hand and his jaw dropped. It was clear that he had at least some idea of its worth.

"Now why would you give him that," I asked as he took me to the old car he had just purchased. "He's certainly going to remember us now."

"Do you really think that either he or his father, if he chooses to share the news of his new riches with him, would tell anyone about that rock? I've pretty much made sure they keep their mouths shut. Whatever the boy does with it, he's not going to flash it around here."

He had a point, so I let it go.

Getting into the little car, I was reminded of some trips I had taken through Paris and the tiny cars they had there. This one, much like the Mercedes I had driven then, gave that same feeling of traveling in a box made of aluminum foil with little wheels attached, but if it got us at least most of the way to Amman, I would be happy. I hoped it had at least close to the same mileage, because if it did, we might come away with fuel to spare.

I reclined my seat and found that it would just about lay flat against the back seat, such as it was. It was nice to be able to do that after riding for so long in a truck equipped with only a bench seat. Reaching around behind Nathaniel, I pulled out a soft blanket that had apparently been included with the sale of the car, and pulled it over myself.

"Glad you found that!" He said to me. "I talked the seller out of it at the last minute. Told him my flower of a wife needed something soft like that to rest with. His eyes got all misty and he practically forced it on me."

"Flower of a wife?" I scoffed. "You're the flower, I think. I'm more of an artichoke."

"I was not going to tell him that," Nathaniel laughed. "I liked the blanket and thought you'd like it as much as I did. Now get some rest. I'll be tossing you in the driver's seat in a bit."

The blanket was clean and smelled of having been hung out in the sun to dry. It was not difficult at all to lose myself in its delightful texture and warmth, and soon I was in a heavy doze.

"Besides, I like you as a prickly flower," I heard him murmur just as I fell asleep.

Three

Nathaniel nudged me awake as we approached some kind of a road block. It was dusk, and the sun was just a sliver of fire on the horizon, bathing the sky in a wash of color. I had always enjoyed colorful sunsets, and this one was no exception. In this case, however, Nathaniel had not awakened me to see the sun go to bed, but to bring something of far more concern to my attention.

"You're going to want to see this," he told me. That washed any lingering sleepiness from my mind immediately. The shit pile had definitely gotten deeper, and I did not like the smell of things one bit.

"Well, shit!" I said bluntly.

Levering my seat back to something fairly upright, but still reasonably comfortable for me, I saw a group of about six armed humans stopping each vehicle ahead of us and either allowing them move on or motioning them to the side, where the humans inside were either dragged away protesting innocence of some perceived crime or simply bullied and then permitted to continue their interrupted journey. Nathaniel was already braking to join the queue arranged before of us on the road.

"Now what are we going to do, Siofra? We haven't had to deal with something like this in front of so many witnesses before. Do we plan to take out everyone, if it comes to that?"

It was a reasonable question, but right now, I had no answers for him. He was right, we'd managed to avoid encounters like this one for the entire time since he had been turned, but never was a long time, and it had just run out on the both of us.

"Let me think for a moment, Nathaniel. I'm hoping we don't have to, but I'm not sure we're going to be that lucky," I replied. "The only question now is about how much damage we're going to take when we hightail it out of here. I'm not sure the car can handle that much damage."

I knew that we did not stand much chance of escaping their notice. There was no way they would believe we were locals, and playing handoff with gems from the medallion would be useless as well. They'd take it away from us and then take us off for torture and whatever else, immediately after they determined we did not have any more shiny baubles for them to confiscate.

There were at least ten vehicles ahead of us, so we had at least a few minutes to figure out what we were going to do.

"I wish off-roading were more of an option for us, but it's just too damned dangerous around here. One well-placed mine, and we'll be singing hosannas for eternity," he noted. "I've never been one for choirs."

"Just look bored. Use that expression you had when you were hunting in Ramadi last month. That one always seems to put humans at ease," I suggested. "They practically line up to shake your hand when you do."

Another three cars were detained, and they let two through. It seemed that several of the ones who were let through knew the guards, at least from the grins I saw on the faces of the thugs who "guarded" the road we were traveling. The sixth car, however – the sixth car changed things. The shouting started almost from the outset and things only escalated from there.

The guard who did the questioning was clearly amped up about something, and appeared to be demanding a lot of information from whoever was behind the wheel. He started to raise his weapon when the driver of car number six gunned his engine and shot forward, leaving the stunned guards scattering in all directions to avoid becoming a casualty. Unfortunately for one of them, he did not move quickly enough to get out of the way, and was thrown about twenty feet from the road. Once he landed, he lay still. I did not even detect breathing.

Shouting orders, the now raging guard gestured for his people to clamber into their own vehicles and they started off after the sixth car, a Hummer that had seen better days. Its rear end was pockmarked with the dents of impacts the size of bullets, so this was something that had happened before. I was just happy to see them all go off in another direction so we could continue on our way to Jordan and relative freedom.

Those of us who had been held up waiting turned our engines back on and got moving once again. No one, innocent or guilty, wanted to find themselves facing armed men who were determined to find new victims. It was not as though these were police officers or soldiers. They were self-appointed guardians of what they deemed to be the public good.

Whether or not their version of "public good" was anything near what that might actually have been. Every culture had them, at one time or another. Even in the most "free" of countries.

"I'm glad someone blinked, Siofra. I'm hungry, but obviously, there were too many humans around to make feeding possible," he said, slumping into his seat once more and driving one-handed, his right arm stretched across the back of my seat, absently playing with my hair with his fingertips. "We should try to find somewhere to feed soon."

"You're right. I can see the lights of some city or village to the northwest, so let's keep heading that way. We can stop there, feed, and then see about finding fuel when we're done," I replied, pointing at the fuel gauge. "It looks like we still have nearly a half tank of fuel, but if we can at least top it off, that wouldn't hurt."

While the glow of light on the horizon had correctly indicated the presence of a town, it still took over an hour to get there. The sun had long ago gone to bed, and taken the glowing horizon with it for a comforter.

At first, we considered parking in town, but decided that was not the best idea. Thus, we concealed the little Mercedes off the road near a thick wedge of scrub and threw some extra dirt onto it for good measure in order to downplay any shine that might reflect from its badly painted exterior.

It was only a few mile walk into town, and we could cover that distance very quickly on foot. There was no sense in driving in and making ourselves even more easily seen. Nathaniel had suggested bringing the gas cans along, but I pointed out that a couple of obvious outsiders walking around with gas cans would bring too much unwanted attention. If we were able to find fuel, we could probably buy cans to put it in while we were there.

I had changed long ago from my blood-spattered clothing, and now sported a pair of loose-fit warm-up pants and long-sleeved cotton tunic. Before we left the car, I added a bulky long-sleeved sweater to my clothing, and then covered my hair and most of my face with a featureless scarf in order to blend in better with the local women. I was not necessarily trying to make myself look like an Iraqi. That would not be something I could ever pull off easier. Instead, I had found that oftentimes, showing modesty from the start in cultures such as this one could help to smooth the way for good relations when it came time to trade.

"So, do I look modest enough, Nathaniel? I'm trying for shapeless. Am I getting that with this?" I asked him, pirouetting for him. He laughed and nodded.

"You could nearly be mistaken for a boy, Siofra," he told me. "Don't glare at me for saying it, either. Looking at way is probably good, considering how touchy some of these people can be about displaying curves."

"It's not my fault that my diet while I was still human was so poor. I don't think I even got my period until I hit my mid to late teens."

"From everything I've read, Siofra, girls did not have pre-teen periods until after the turn of the last century. It all has to do with how well nourished a human child is, as to what age her bits mature," he intoned.

"*Bits*? Oh, come on, Nathaniel. You can do better than that!" I erupted. "I can't believe you called them *bits*."

He bowed floridly, his right arm describing an arc as though he were doffing a hat to me.

"My deepest apologies, my lady! Your pardon for my offensive wording!" He intoned, sounding like a renaissance faire refugee.

I stalked away, shaking my head, not waiting for him to catch up. He would whenever he felt like it, anyway. Sometimes, engaging in conversation with Nathaniel could sometimes seem as though I was trying to debate a six year old human child. When those situations became too much for me, I often sought something resembling solitude, and Nathaniel had learned to respect that.

For now, he knew I was irritated, and so left me to myself for the time being. I knew he would be at my side by the time fifteen minutes was up, so I simply ignored him. It was not anything I had not done in the past.

I hope you haven't been living under the assumption that Nathaniel's and my relationship was all songbirds and smooth sailing, because, as with any relationship, it had its ups and downs. That's normal. Hell, I did things that annoyed the hell out of him as well. There's a reason why, in most cases, vampires tend to remain loners, and only a few have a strong enough relationship that causes them to marry, such as was the case with Janos and Estella. Imagine what a marriage can be like when both of you have the potential to be around for several hundred years. If "familiarity breeds contempt", as the saying goes, what's it like after a hundred years, much less three or four hundred years?

"Sorry, Siofra. My sense of humor got the best of me," Nathaniel said, when he finally lengthened his stride in order to catch up with me. "I should know by now that you don't like it."

"You know I prefer to avoid the slang, Nathaniel," I responded. "That should not be a surprise."

"I know, and again, I'm sorry."

I looked up at the young vampire walking beside me and took his hand in my own.

"I know you are, and I know you'll do it again," I said. "I probably should not let it bother me so much, since that's just the way you are, and I should realize that by now."

He squeezed my hand in response, but did not say a word. He knew I would get ticked off at him again, sure as two economists in the same room are like matter and anti-matter having a pow-wow. It was a long time before he said anything to me, his words almost cautious, as though he expected me to explode at him.

"I know you've told me some of what your life was like as a human, Siofra. I guess being from a time where children in the West generally get enough to eat, I really don't have experience relating to what you went through. I should be more sensitive, and I was not."

"Its okay, Nathaniel. To some degree, I guess I have a bit of a thin skin. There are good things and bad things to being what we are. Unchanging immortality is great, to some degree, but there are some things that will never change," I said. "You're lucky you had muscle development before I turned you, otherwise, no matter how much you might work out, you'd never develop it now. You know how muscle mass is created, correct?"

"Ya. Working out tears your muscles and the healing process gives you a bulkier look," he said. Then his eyes widened. "Oh. It'd just heal back the way it had been, so the classic fifty-pound-weakling will always look that way."

"Exactly. On the other hand, there are some vampires out there who look like the fifty-pound-weaklings they used to be, and so it's easy for a human to misjudge their opponent. Just as people have misjudged me over the centuries, to their own detriment. There are good things and bad things about this unchanging aspect we possess."

"I never thought about it before now. I just thought I was keeping busy enough that I had not lost what I'd gained," he said. "I worked so hard on it after the doctors said I was in remission."

He had told me long ago about his battle with leukemia, and how it had been in remission for about five years by the time he had become a vampire. I had never told him that I had been able to taste the cancer in his blood that night, and did not think it would help if I told him that all these years later. He would have started showing visible symptoms soon, if he had not first met his death that night so long ago. Once he had become a vampire, disease would never touch him again. His cancer was not in remission now, it was gone completely.

There's a kind of irony to fighting against a cancer of the blood and then becoming a vampire. I don't know if he had ever seen the humor in it, but I certainly did.

"You can work out if it makes you feel better, but no, your body will neither gain nor lose muscle mass. It can recede temporarily, if you go too long without feeding, but once you feed again, it'll all bulk up once more," I said.

Nathaniel had never really been without feeding for very long, except for his first feeding. After that event, we'd both been very careful to be sure he fed as often as possible. His loss of control had frightened him, and he had confided in me that he never wanted to experience such a terrible loss of self control again. At this point in his existence, he could go for about three to four days before he started to feel the pull to find a human from whom to feed. That was not enough time to make him look scary to the average human, but he would start looking a bit ill to the casual observer.

"By the same token, someone who is turned while they are overweight will spend their existence as an overweight vampire. It's not going to hurt them to be overweight, but they'll never lose it." I noted. "Vampires come in all shapes and sizes."

"I'm just glad we're not expected to walk around in formal clothing, like you see in the movies," Nathaniel said, chuckling. "I would say I'm more the tee shirt and jeans variety of vampire."

"I came from the time of corsets, gowns and all that frippery, and I'm not into it either, Nathaniel. I would rather be comfortable, and the clothing of my human life was anything but that." I told him. "As soon as I was able, once I was turned, I spent most of my time dressed as a man until I needed to appear feminine."

We arrived in the village to find an ebb and flow of activity. We'd apparently shown up just before the next call to prayer. Shopkeepers appeared to be closing up shop for the evening, putting things away and locking up their storefronts. It was a good time to hunt.

The streets were mostly empty once the majority of the humans were wherever they went to wash up and then pray the *Isha'*, which is the last prayer of the day. It gave Nathaniel and me the opportunity to look around and see if there was anything useful around that we could take with us.

We'd brought the backpack with the laptops in it, in the event our vehicle was discovered. There was no point in leaving them behind. Our papers, on the other hand, were buried under one of the shrubs near where we'd left the car. No sense in having everything all in one place. Janos had taught me that shortly after we'd first met.

As the last human in line disappeared into the mosque, we waited another few minutes in the event someone was late getting to prayer. A heavily bearded human male stood at the door, waiting patiently, and I heard him laugh quietly to himself as a teenage boy, bright green sneakers sticking out incongruously from his otherwise traditional garb, and keffiyeh flapping in the wind of his run, nearly tumbled into the doorway.

Seeing the adult standing on the stoop, the boy, sporting what could only be called 'baby beard' came to a halt. He greeted the adult respectfully and then apologized for his tardiness. I had the feeling this was a common occurrence between the boy and this particular adult human.

Stern-faced, the adult responded with a gentle admonition that being on time was the respectful thing to do, and the child stammered his reassurances that this would never happen again. A simple wordless raised eyebrow from the adult indicated his doubt at the youngster's promise, but he nodded once and then they both walked into the mosque, the adult male closing the door behind them.

"Reminds me of my old biology instructor in high school," Nathaniel told me as we turned away. "Once that door was closed, the only way you were allowed in was if you had a note from the office. He was a strict old bastard, but only because he wanted you in class to learn. I did not see it that way at the time, though."

"That kid was lucky. The priest at the last place I lived while I was still human would beat us if we were late to the afternoon mass he held in the private chapel on Sundays. He had a thick leather strap set aside for such occasions." I noted. "Someone split him up the middle the night I died. I found him later when the crows were eating his eyes out of his skull. I'd have felt bad about it, I suppose, but I was more interested in finding my next meal at that point."

"From what you've said, a lot of people died that night," he observed. "Do you think anyone survived the attack?"

"If anyone did, they somehow managed to slip out either during the course of the attack or hid out until everyone was gone. There was a priest-hole on the property, but I found no one in there when I went to look. I do have my doubts."

"We don't have a lot of time, and not everyone will be praying right now, so we still have to be careful," I said. It was not anything Nathaniel would not know after several years living in Muslim countries, but it still felt right to say it aloud. "First and foremost, we need to find a good location from which to hunt. If we can use the element of surprise, it should make things go more quickly. I don't like delaying any longer than we absolutely must."

"Are you sure that you want to hunt out in the open? We could probably have our pick from one of the houses here," Nathaniel suggested. "Who knows who might come around the corner at any given time?"

He had a point. I could hear praying from inside some of the other buildings in town, and considered entering and choosing my prey from there, but decided that doing something along those lines was potentially more risky than simply lying in wait outdoors.

"True, however, you know as well as I do that not everyone prays at exactly the same time. As long as they pray by a certain time, they're covered," I replied. "It's not the whole 'its 9am, time for church' thing when it comes to their Call to Prayer."

For now, we moved from the ground to the roofs of the buildings, looking for a likely vantage point from which to find prey. We could not drag this out, since we needed to get back on the road and get to Amman before another day had passed. The wait at the Iraqi-Jordan border would be a nightmare. The last I had heard was that it was easily a six hour wait to get through the line of traffic we'd find when we got there.

Four

It was all so sudden that even with our heightened reflexes, we were unable to avoid being caught in the resulting chaos. One moment, we were crouched alongside the rear wall of the building, waiting for supper to saunter by, and the next, Hell's doors swung wide and released its sulfurous exhalation, lighting up the night in yellow, orange and blue flame.

Actually, it was some kind of bomb that went off, but the resulting heat was...well...hellish.

The explosion threw us both through the air and I was painfully pinned to the ground by the resulting debris from the demolished building. I had endured similar situations in the past, but this time, unlike the others, I was pinned like a butterfly to a display board, with no way to free myself.

There appeared to be a couple hundred pound chunk of cement lying across my shoulders and mid-back area that kept me from moving. If this had happened with one of my extremities, I could have gone so far as to break free and simply feed to regrow it, but that was not going to happen in this situation. My ears still rang from the shock wave, so it was almost impossible for me to hear anything else around me, which was almost frightening.

I knew that I would recover my hearing quickly, but that did not help to ease my fears. I shouted Nathaniel's name, but of course was unable to hear if he even responded to me. For all I knew, debris could have ended him with a well-placed piece of cement to the skull or an impromptu shrapnel guillotine to the neck. Until I could hear his voice or see him, however, I had no chance of knowing if he was still with me.

The air was choked with dust, smoke and asbestos, as a result of the explosion. In my case, I was so very happy that I did not have to breathe anymore, as I might otherwise have been poisoned or even killed by the crap that now floated through the air, looking for a place to land. As it was, fine dust particles were stuck to my eyeballs, and my tears were having a hard time washing them clean once more, so my eyesight was a bit muzzy.

My concern now, though, was to find a way to wrest myself loose from my prison and then find Nathaniel, if he did not manage to find me first.

The first inkling I had that my hearing was returning came as I began to hear the sounds of people running about, looking for bodies, survivors and any conveniently unguarded loot that might be on the ground. I grunted as I felt a hand in a back pocket and was gratified to hear a shout of surprise and then the sound of more feet running toward me.

There was a rumble of noise, and then someone yanked hard at my hair, quickly followed by a raise in volume. I think I heard the word "red" in there, somewhere, but I could have been mistaken. As long as no one yanked any of it out, I had a chance at escaping into the night. If they did and saw what happened to that hair, they'd probably add several more stones to the ones that pinned me to the ground, an unlikely butterfly in someone's gruesome collection.

Someone else with a heavy step approached, and I felt my hands being yanked behind me and then what could only be the cold iron of manacles being affixed to my wrists. The same was done to my ankles, despite my efforts to kick them away. I was like a turtle on its back, helpless and at the mercy of these humans who had no idea what they were getting themselves into.

I was still unable to really grasp the meaning of the words being shouted around me. I knew my hearing would recover, for now, I did not know how long that would take. I could tell that the humans were excited and angry, but that was it for now.

Only after I had been secured did I feel them work to remove the weight from my back. Perhaps three of them got a handhold under it and then lifted it away from me. The cessation of the heavy weight on my body was a relief, but I wondered how I would get free of the bonds that kept me from escaping or even defending myself.

Did I forget to mention that fact?

Unless you find a way to keep me from using my hands and feet, I can generally do a pretty good job of defending myself and ending you in the process. For now, I was at the mercy of the humans who held me, and I had better do a damned good job of passing for human if I wanted any slight chance at survival. I could only hope that I was not injured enough that they might make note of the fact that I did not bleed correctly.

Once they had removed the debris from my body and a cursory check was made to be sure I was still among the living, I was rudely jerked to my feet and forced to start walking. I was careful to pretend to breathe as I went. It would not do to have someone notice that I was neither inhaling nor exhaling.

My hearing was finally returning, so I was able to follow some of the conversations around me. I did not like the tone of what I was hearing, as it was evident that whatever had happened, I was their prime suspect in all of it.

One of the humans kept stroking my hair, seeming fascinated by it. I saw him fingering his knife and prayed that he would not think to cut some off as a trophy. That alone would mark me as being something other than human, when the cut hair went white and then crumbled into a fine dust.

"Do not touch the infidel's hair, Hassam!" admonished one of my other captors. "It should be properly covered, so as to be modest."

With that, he pulled a piece of cloth from a pocket and coiled my hair up inside it before tying it, kerchief-style, behind my head. I was surprised that he even cared about enforcing my modesty, but perhaps this would be an opportunity to get free of my bonds under the guise of relieving myself. My hopes were short-lived, as another scrap of cloth was produced and I was quickly blindfolded.

"You don't need to do that!" I told them, but the blindfold remained.

"Were there any others found in the ruins," the one who apparently held my wrists asked. "Salleh said that he thought there may have been at least one other."

"Yes, we have also captured another. He has already been taken to the camp and we will join them there. There is concern that they had something to do with the bombing of the school."

Oh, shit. It was a school, and now they thought we were involved? This was not going well at all!

"Is everyone at the school okay?" I managed in their own language. We came to a sudden halt, and the one who had put the kerchief on my head jerked my head up by the chin. His eyes were a very dark brown, and his long wavy hair pulled back in a queue. It appeared that he probably had not shaved in all the time since hair had first begun to sprout on his chin and cheeks. I was surprised that he was not wearing a *keffiyeh*, but he obviously had his reasons for the omission.

"By the grace of God, there was no one in the building," he breathed, allowing relief to color his words. "Who are you and what are you doing here? Why did you bomb the building?"

"I did not bomb the building. I'm just trying to get through to Jordan and be on my way," I replied. Honestly was probably the best tack here, since it was easier to remember it. Nathaniel and I had long ago decided that this was best, in the event we were ever separated and interrogated. That way, there was no notable difference in whatever story we told anyone who asked. "My friend and I were walking past the building when the explosion happened. Have you seen him? He's taller than me, light eyes, brown wavy hair, and very light skin like mine."

That last brought an involuntary chuckle from one of the men who held me. The dust from the explosion had colored my skin more of a gray tone than anything resembling my normal pale complexion. This actually darkened my skin quite a bit, making me appear less odd than I already did. I was now as grey-complected as a cinema zombie, but I looked more human than I might otherwise.

"Your comrade has been apprehended and his interrogation may have begun already," I was told. "Confess your crimes now, and you may live."

"I haven't done anything wrong!"

"For what other reason could you have been skulking around outside the school, then?"

"We were only walking!" I protested. That was close enough to the truth. Of course, what remained unsaid was that we had been walking very slowly as we waited for a likely meal or two to come conveniently by. That information would undoubtedly be received quite poorly.

I was answered with a blow to the back of the head and shut my mouth. Not surprisingly, they'd already come to a conclusion as to my involvement in the explosion and were planning to torture me into admitting to it. Of course, anyone will confess to something, if only to make the torture stop and the pain go away. I had been around long enough to know that to be true.

We walked a while longer, and then I was shoved into a waiting vehicle which drove away at a high rate of speed. Wherever we were going, it was some distance from where this had all started. My abductors talked amongst themselves in low whispers, obviously observant of my previous example of not only knowing, but speaking their language.

At least they were unaware of my enhanced hearing ability, so I was able to follow their conversation.

It seemed that "the big male American" was being closed-mouthed, except in his demands to see me, alive and unharmed. They seemed convinced that they could use me as a tool to get him to talk, so they would let him see me, and then begin hurting me in order to get him to reveal whatever it was they thought he knew.

There was no way they would let either of us go free. One of the humans started talking about beheading us and taking a video of it to "send to the Americans so they will know we are serious". In the state I was in now, I was in no position to defend myself in the event they decided to do just that.

I had only been restrained this way once before, and that was almost three hundred years ago. I had only escaped after I coaxed my jailer into making a rash decision and removing the shackle from one of my wrists. There was no way I was going to be as successful convincing these humans to do the same thing. They were not looking for sex from me. They were looking for terror.

Sometime later, the car came to an abrupt halt and I was hauled out of the trunk and half-dragged into a building of some sort. Inhaling deeply, I caught the smell of livestock and rotting flesh and blood. This was not going to be good.

Five

"**A**llan?!" I called out.

"Mitzi!" was Nathaniel's gratifying reply. I really should make sure I have more control over the names that are put on potential fake papers. I am *so* not a "Mitzi". It was all perhaps Janos' last very bad joke at my expense. The name "Mitzi" has always sounded perky to me, and I despise perkiness. I know we did not have our papers with us, but I found it best to keep up the disguise, just in case something unexpected occurred.

There was the thick sound of flesh hitting flesh, and then a burst of profanity as Nathaniel responded in a typically male fashion to the blow. I knew that if he had the opportunity, Nathaniel would make that human suffer for having struck him. Trying to defend oneself was one thing, but straight blind violence for its own sake was something else entirely.

"Where are we, Allan? What's going on?" I could sound airheaded and clueless when the opportunity presented itself. This seemed to be one of those times. "I can't see you. They've got me blindfolded."

The blindfold in question was suddenly ripped from my face and I blinked to stretch my formerly uncomfortably compressed eyelids and bring the room into focus. I gasped in shock. Any hope I might have entertained of our potential escape was dashed when I saw that he was bound hand and foot, just as I had been.

Nathaniel was on his knees, head bowed. A heavily muscled human stood in front of him, looking as though he was eagerly awaiting his opportunity to land his next blow on the helpless man in front of him. My reaction was to try to fight my way free, but instead, the manacles cut into my flesh, and I had to stop myself before I did enough damage to myself that it was noticeable. While they thought we were human, we had time. If they discovered we were something other than human, I doubted we'd see another five minutes of existence.

I stumbled forward, the chain that joined both of my ankle manacles keeping my step short and off-balance. Surprisingly, they allowed me to fall against him.

"They're going to kill us, regardless of the answers we give them," I muttered to him. "I don't know how the hell we're going to get out of this. As long as we're shackled like this, there's nothing we can do to protect ourselves."

"I know," was his reply. "I'm sorry that I thought we should take the time to feed. It's all my fault."

"The hell it is! We had no idea that something like this could happen, and I don't think there was any way we could have planned for it," I consoled him. "At least I got to meet you, Nathaniel Ian Bock."

"Nathaniel Ian O'Se, thank you very much," he admonished me. "It's been fun."

Something inside me swelled up as he acknowledged our kinship, even at this terrible time. Perhaps it was stupid of me to feel so touched by his words when we were facing our ends, but I had no control over how it made me feel.

Two of the humans dragged me away from Nathaniel, but not so far that we lost sight of one another. A third human attacked my chains to another ring on the floor. It was obvious that they wanted him to see whatever it was they were planning to do to me. Sadistic bastards, one and all. I wished there was some way I would be able to take out at least a few of them before they ended me, but that was a wildly unlikely prospect.

When the one who had dragged me away tore my shirt off of me, I screamed in shock. It doesn't matter when you're a vampire. Rape is still rape. Nathaniel roared with rage, and tried to break free, but I saw that they had actually chained him to the floor. He was not going anywhere anytime soon. The bastard who held me remarked on the paleness of my skin, and ran his hand down my breasts and belly. A conspicuous lump below his waist let me know that doing this aroused him.

"Leave her alone!" he shouted at them. "We don't know anything about what happened!"

"We don't believe you," was the reply. "You Americans are into everything, and have no respect for our culture. Tell us what we want to know and we will set you free."

"I don't know what you want," Nathaniel protested. "We don't know anything about the explosion!"

"Who are you? Why do you not have identification papers on you," the human in charge demanded. "If you have nothing to hide, why do you not have passports on you?"

"They were stolen from us a few days ago, and we were trying to find someone who could help us replace them," was Nathaniel's reply.

"Tell us who you are and we will help you with your papers," his interrogator purred.

The carnivorous smile he gave was swathed in sincerity, while deceit danced in his dark eyes. He had told this lie before in this room, and the stench it held had poisoned the air with its evil. I wondered how many people had heard this lie before and believed it, and then how many had heard it and seen past the sincere smile and seen their death in those bright eyes.

My captor tore my jeans down off my hips and down to my knees, knocking me over backward onto the ground, the edges of the manacles cutting further into my skin. I could feel moisture oozing out and down between the metal of the manacles and my flesh. It would only be a matter of time before they noticed I was not human, and then I would be seeing Janos again, but not in a happy way.

I screamed and writhed under him. It seemed to be what he wanted to see and hear, and the longer I could keep him distracted, the longer it would take for him to know I was not human. I pleaded with him, and out of the corner of my eye, I could see Nathaniel throwing himself against the chain that held him to a thick ring set into the cement floor. His minder laughed and beat Nathaniel about the head and shoulders, but Nathaniel did not pay attention to the abuse.

"Let her go!" he screamed at them. The sheer volume of his voice got their attention, and they looked at him in shock and maybe something like terror. "Let her go now or so help me—"

"Tell us who planned this with you, and we will set her free," reiterated the one who had been beating him. That human had moved a few feet away from Nathaniel, and I saw something like fear in his eyes. He was beginning to realize there was something different about the people they were interrogating, but he could not yet quantify it.

"I told you, we don't know anything!"

For some reason, at that point, the human stabbed Nathaniel in the meat of his left bicep arm with the jagged-edged knife I had seen slipped into the belt at his waist. Nathaniel cursed, but did not flinch. The human's eyes widened as they saw a stain of black fluid begin to color the fabric of Nathaniel's cotton shirt.

"Devil!" he gasped, pointing at the evidence of Nathaniel's inhuman self and then stabbing him in the other arm for good measure. "See, he does not bleed as we do! His black soul is trying to break free!"

The one who had been trying to rape me looked down at me as though for the first time. An expression of horror crossed his face, and he could not get off me fast enough. He drew his own knife and held it out between us as though it were some talisman that would protect him from whatever it was he thought he faced.

"We must destroy these devils before they escape and do more damage," muttered the one who faced Nathaniel. He walked to a back table and grabbed up a hacksaw with a filthy blade, then returned to where Nathaniel raged. "Salleh, Omar, come and hold it, so I may remove its head and then burn it. That is the only way to destroy devils!"

It was my turn to begin to rage. I clumsily got to my feet and tried to lunge at the one who held the hacksaw at Nathaniel's neck. It was a pathetic attempt, overall, but at least it gained Nathaniel some more time as the suddenness and violence of my reaction distracted them. Agony shot through my arms and shoulders as I continued to throw myself against the chains that held me, but they were strong enough to withstand the beating I put them through.

Once they realized I was not an immediate threat, the humans moved to encircle Nathaniel, each holding a weapon of one sort or another. I tried screaming at them from where I was chained, saying whatever came to mind to try to distract them, but they continued to ignore me, as I was not a threat to them in my current condition. I became even more frantic, trying as hard as I could to work myself free, and tearing the flesh from my wrists as I did, spilling my own bodily fluids all over myself and the floor.

Sadly, the manacles were too well-kept to break easily, and all I managed to do was damage myself further. Nathaniel's scream as they applied the hacksaw to his neck and began their grisly task made my mind go blank and I screamed along with him in my frustration and anguish at being unable to save him.

It was then that the door to the livestock barn opened, and a dark-cloaked figure entered. The humans who previously had focused their attention on Nathaniel were finally distracted from their task, and moved to confront the stranger. From their expressions, I could tell they were unfamiliar with him, and did not know how to handle the newcomer.

"What is going on here?" I heard a soft voice from inside the concealing folds of the cloak's hood. The piece of clothing concealed the stranger utterly and making his presence even that more intimidating to the humans. "What have these people done to deserve such harsh treatment?"

"Who are you to ask us questions? How dare you enter this place and stick your nose in where it doesn't belong?" This was from the one who had so recently been trying to rape me. He stepped away to reveal Nathaniel and the gruesome wound he had created in the side of this throat. Looking at the extent of the damage, I knew that it would only be a matter of a few more passes of the thin blade before his neck would be severed. The hacksaw appeared to have just hit the vertebrae of his neck, and I sent up a silent thanks to anyone or anything that might have been paying attention.

Black ooze stained the lips of the wound and had trickled down onto Nathaniel's shirt. The human gestured broadly at Nathaniel, his dark eyes wide and his face twisted in disgust.

"Can you not see we are dealing with devils?" He asked in an otherwise reasonable-sounding tone of voice. "How many more of the Americans are demons?"

"Ah, yes. I thought I smelled something familiar," said the voice of the currently unknown visitor. "You really should not do things like that. It rarely ends well, you know."

Now it was time for the thugs to look uncertain, but the one who was preparing to end Nathaniel tried on some bravado to see if it would have any effect on the stranger. He puffed himself up and made himself look as though he had some importance. It did not work very well at all, really.

"We are part of the local militia and were looking into the explosion in town, and discovered these American infidels who had been caught in the blast. They are obviously responsible for destroying the school!" He insisted. "In the course of interrogating them, we discovered that they are not even human. They are demons!"

And he gestured at the black fluid that now stained Nathaniel's arm from his right bicep to his wrist. I mentally ran through a string of profanity that might have made a telepath blush.

"If you had stayed long enough, you would have learned that the explosion was caused by a faulty water heater in the school," said the stranger amiably, seemingly unmoved by what he had been shown. "You kidnapped and interrogated these persons for no reason at all."

"But, they are demons! We must protect our community from they who would destroy our families and our way of life!" Exclaimed the human. "Surely you can understand that!"

And then the stranger pushed the cloak's hood back and smiled at our captors. Shoulder-length wavy hair the color of ebony was pulled away from his bearded face and bound with a leather thong, a stark contrast to his pale grey eyes. Faintly red lips contrasted against skin that was at least as pale as my own, framing a pair of shining ivory fangs that caught the attention of the humans in the room.

"If they are demons, then what does that make me," he asked in a kind of purr. He shrugged his cloak from off of his shoulders, allowing it to fall to the ground. He was revealed to be wearing loose cotton trousers and a similarly loose blouse, both jet black in color, matching the crumpled cloak that lay on the ground behind him. The stranger sketched a bow to the stunned humans in the room, a mocking smile on his face.

The first scream rang out and everything became a bit of a blur.

The humans never stood a chance. They felt like big men when facing chained monsters, but when the monster stood right in front of them, unfettered, they were too shocked and frightened to assay a defense. All the better if it would save Nathaniel and me from the gruesome ending that had been promised us.

The strange vampire moved about the room like the consummate martial artist, striking out with hands, feet, knees and elbows, rendering all four of the humans unconscious in the process. I had not seen anything like that before, and something told me I never would again. I knew it had taken a surprising amount of control to keep from simply ending the humans completely, and was not sure I would have been able to simply render them comatose in the same circumstances.

"I...who...?" I was just about wordless in my relief.

"Now," he said, as he surveyed the carnage. "Let's see about getting you two unchained and out of here. There are people looking for you, Siofra O'Se. If you dawdle much longer, they may yet find you."

Six

"**W**ho are you? How do you know my name?" I finally found my voice as he took what appeared to be a skeleton key from the back table and proceeded to remove my chains, and then Nathaniel's. "I don't know you."

"Well, we have never actually met, young lady, but I saw your picture once," he replied. His voice had a slightly musical-sounding lilt that made me think of old Ireland, but there was a quality to it that was not quite Gaelic. I wondered if I would have the chance to find out where he was from, originally. Vampire culture frowned upon that kind of nosiness. "It was a little while after you bought your little red roadster. Lovely vehicle. Automobiles these days are so monotonous, compared with the old days, I think."

My little red roadster. I had torn up and down the hills and valleys of old Los Angeles in that thing, top down and not a care in the world. It had been my first automobile, and so had a very warm spot in my memories.

"Who are you," I repeated. "How could you remember me from such a brief glance at a picture of me?"

He rewarded me with a quirky smile and inclined his head in my direction, never taking his eyes from mine. They were very old eyes, not matching the youth of his appearance, and I was faced with yet another mystery. A vampire's eyes slowly lighten over the centuries, and his were quite light at this point in his existence, but there was also a wisdom in his eyes.

"Ah, my apologies. I am Fáolán," he said. "I have what is called in this time an 'eidetic memory'. I remember everything I experience."

"Everything?" Nathaniel asked, walking over to one of our former tormentors and proceeding to gorge on his blood. "That's amazing! What a gift!"

"It is no gift," he told Nathaniel flatly, disgust on his face. "It is a curse. I remember everything that has happened to me since I first became aware of myself, and that was over one thousand years ago. I'll even recall this little interlude between the three of us and these humans, including our conversation."

"Everything?" I asked, awed. Gobsmacked, really. I'd heard of what was wrongly referred to as photographic memories, but had never before encountered someone who actually had one.

"Everything. As I said, this is no gift. Would you wish to exist more than a thousand years and remember everything you had ever experienced, said or heard? That is my existence."

"One thousand?!" was my shocked response. "I've never met anyone as old as you!"

That statement sounded really bad, even to my own ears, and I wished I could have found some other way to acknowledge him without making him sound like he was downright ancient. Well, he was, but it was impolite to comment on the fact.

"There are not many who are even close to my age," he allowed. "Now, I know you, but who is this young man? I have heard nothing of you having a companion."

"This is Nathaniel," I said. "I turned him several years ago and decided it was safer to teach him about what he had become somewhere that a few more bodies lying around wouldn't necessarily garner too much attention. We've been here ever since, and really haven't met any other vampires here until you in that time. The ones who tried to end me thought he was my boyfriend or something. They did not know he was my fledgling."

"End you?"

"We were in a seedy old hotel and were attacked by four assassins. They were vampires and apparently had come at the bidding of someone else. I can only assume it was the Council," I told him. "We managed to end three of them and let one leave."

"You let one of them leave? That doesn't seem to be the wisest thing you could have done, young lady," he chided me. "An enemy left behind is a vampire who could come back and finish what he started."

"I was not too worried about letting him go. He was badly wounded and knew that I could have ended him easily, rather than letting him leave," I said. "I may be expecting too much, but I'd like to think he feels at least some small debt to me in letting him go."

"Whatever you've done is on your head," he said. "You must live with the consequences your actions will create."

"You're right. He may have gone back and said 'we failed', but I suspect that he's not in a position to go back to his masters having been unsuccessful. Yes, I could be wrong with that, but from what I recall of the Council, they don't tolerate failure one bit."

The older vampire gave me a twisted smile and a short nod of acceptance.

"Anyway," he said," I cannot stay here, as the Council is looking for me. I escaped them a few years ago, and I know they will not rest until they once again have me captive."

"Why would they want to keep you captive?" Nathaniel asked him.

"Ah, yes, well, they keep me around to remember what has happened," he replied. "I have been privy to every Council meeting since shortly after I was turned. Well, except for those times when I have been fortunate enough to free myself."

"Free yourself? I don't understand." Nathaniel said.

"I was a young man in ancient Britain when Roman vampires discovered my curse. They apparently decided that someone with such a thing should be made a vampire to be bent to their purposes, and so they did," there was an aching loss in his voice that tore at me. "Once they had turned me and bound me with my first feeding, they whisked me away on one of their ships and I never saw my family again."

"If you've lived this long and can remember everything you've seen and heard, you must have a lot of stories to tell," Nathaniel observed. "Have you chronicled the things you've seen?"

"No," he replied. "There are those on the Council who do not like to have things written down, thus they rely on me to remember everything for them. I have seen the makeup of the Council change several times over my existence, but most all of them shun modern technology. Even something as minor as a tape recorder."

"That's just stupid," I said, having finished my own feeding. My would-be rapist had been delicious. "If something happened to you, they would lose all of that, anyway!"

"That is true, Siofra, however, they have done all they can to keep me safe and as healthy as a vampire may possibly be. I imagine they must panic when I flee them. They are running out of ways to keep me captive as I learn how to defeat the bonds they place upon me."

I said nothing, simply allowing his words to sink in.

"Let us go, Siofra and Nathaniel. While it was true that the explosion was caused by a faulty water heater, there was evidence that it had been tampered with, and the authorities are now searching for suspects. *Any* suspects. It is only a matter of time before someone comes to investigate what has happened here," he said, covering his face once again with his hood and going to the door. "So grab whatever possessions of yours mean something to you and come with me."

"How did you even find us?" I wondered aloud as I grabbed my now-filthy backpack from the table and shoved the remains of our laptops into it. Fáolán was busy emptying the contents of a brazier onto a pile of rags and other burnables, which obligingly began smoking as they worked their way into becoming a merry blaze. "I did not even know there was another vampire in the area."

"I suppose you could call it blind luck. I have been staying here in this town for the past few weeks, disguised as a tinker. I have kept to myself, except when I would go to feed. I only discovered you because I varied from my normal routine. I had planned to go into town to feed, but instead, I chose to go for a long walk. If I had followed my first choice, you would both be ended by now," he said quietly as we walked out into the night together, closing the door behind us and concealing the glow of the growing fire, at least until it managed to burn through the wooden walls. "I was able to scent your presence when they did enough damage to one of you that I was able to smell the ichor that fills us."

Ichor? Interesting word choice, but it was certainly better than trying to describe it as "blood", as that was the last thing you could call it. I made a note to try to remember it.

Remember it. Wow. I was overcome with shock and dismay as I thought of a vampire existing for a thousand years and remembering each kill, each encounter, aroma, scream and anything else that might occur within his sphere of kenning. I felt an odd respect for such a vampire, that he had not gone insane from all that horror, always there and waiting like a hungry dog for the cue to come to the fore.

"But for your diversion, we would have been ended and that would have been it for the both of us. I thank whatever gods must have been guiding you that you found us," I said earnestly. "I don't recall ever being quite so close to bidding goodbye to the world."

"I abandoned all gods when they continued to ignore my pleas for an ending," Fáolán replied. "If they don't care about me, why should I care about them?"

"An ending?" Nathaniel asked. "Why would you want an ending? Don't you want to exist as long as you possibly can?"

"Yes, an ending. I cannot continue to exist in this way. I remember each and every encounter I have ever had. Every conversation I have ever heard. Every kill..." his voice faded out, but I could feel his unspoken pain as he remembered.

Remembered. If I had still been capable of doing so, I would have vomited. He was right. It was not a blessing, it was a curse. A terrible, thankless curse. Glancing at Nathaniel, I saw a sick expression cross his face as he realized the horror that had been visited on this vampire for at least a thousand years now. Each tiny bit of Fáolán's entire existence, right there in his memory to pull up and experience all over again, forgetting none of it and being unable to even have them dim as the years and centuries passed.

I realized at that moment what a blessing it was to be able to forget things. Would I have been able to keep my own sanity if I had had to remember each miniscule detail of the last four hundred years? I had my doubts.

"I was not thinking, Fáolán. I'm sorry," Nathaniel apologized to the ancient vampire. "Just the thought of what you've gone through makes me feel queasy."

Fáolán nodded his head, but said nothing. I could see that he was thinking hard about something, but did not inquire. It simply was not any of my business. If he wanted me to know, he would share, but I was not going to be the one to push it.

"Thank you for taking the time to investigate, Fáolán," Nathaniel told him earnestly, breaking the silence. "Neither of us is ready to go, but if we were in your shoes, we might feel differently."

"I am trying to decide now how I will end myself. Simply immolating myself or destroying my brain in some random manner will not do," he told us as we continued to walk. "I cannot tolerate this any longer."

I was shocked at his announcement. The sheer idea of a vampire, someone who was essentially an immortal, wanting to end themselves was something almost impossible to consider. What a loss this would be to our entire community!

"How can you do this without first writing everything down, Fáolán? Have you considered that at all?" I demanded. Pretty cheeky of me to be so demanding, now that I think about it, but the idea that all of that accumulated knowledge and experience being lost was enough to make me forget about manners and respect and made me speak from my innermost self.

"I have been privy to the Council's inner workings, Siofra. I have seen their cruelty, and heard it, even when I was mad with hunger," he replied. "I have been kept chained to a wall while they conducted their interrogations and their meetings. Even those of which they might not want a record kept. I have had enough of all that."

"If you were chained to a wall, how did you manage to escape?" Nathaniel wanted to know. "We wouldn't have been able to get free of the predicament you just witnessed without your help."

"I have some friends," he responded. "They are not always able to intervene on my behalf, but they do what they can, when they can. This time, I have been free for about two months. I almost ended myself my first day out in the world this time, but again, I decided there must be some class, some finesse, to my ending."

"Fáolán, please consider writing your vast store of knowledge down before you finally do end yourself. This is stuff that would otherwise be lost, and you seem an honorable person," I pleaded with him. "If we are successful and are able to end the assholes that are after us now, I'll do everything I can to help you. Provided you are willing to spend the time to write everything down. After a thousand years, what's another hundred or two hundred years to make sure things aren't lost. You have a somewhat unique experience with history, as you well know."

He stopped in his tracks and then looked at me for a long time, considering my words. He opened his mouth once or twice, as though he would say something, but no words came.

"You have hit my sore spot, young lady," he finally said. "One way or another, what I have heard is a part of history. You may recall that famous homily in regard to history, yes?"

"Those who forget history are doomed to repeat it?" Nathaniel and I said in somewhat ragged unison.

"Exactly. You have given me much to consider," he admitted, shaking his head, although in sadness or resignation, I could not tell you. He started walking once again, clasping my upper arm in one hand and pulling me along. "We must keep moving, Siofra and Nathaniel."

We kept moving toward the Mercedes, where it should still be resting under its coating of sand and brush. Conversation was infrequent, even between Nathaniel and me. Fáolán's melancholy had grabbed us all and taken our normal friendly banter away. After a while, however, he did begin to speak again.

"It was not just listening to everything that happened in their chambers, you understand. They would also come and tell me of everything that was happening in the world as they knew it then. They were not interested in writing anything down, for fear of its discovery, but still wanted to have some record of what had transpired," he said. "Have you ever read the book 'Fahrenheit 451'?"

"I read it when I was in junior high," Nathaniel replied. "Very disturbing stuff."

"I've read it also," I said. "The idea of books being banned in their entirety was terrifying to me."

"Indeed. The most efficient way to control a society is to discourage creative thinking skills. In the novel, those in power were able to control their people by removing all references to the past," Fáolán continued. "I have wondered if that is what some in the Council have in mind. Orellos certainly felt that way, before I had the pleasure of ending him."

"You ended Orellos? He was one of the old ones!" I exclaimed. "Well, old as far as I was concerned until now."

Orellos had been an Old World Czechoslovakian vampire who still mourned the bad old days, when the majority of the population labored for the privileged few. He also felt that females, either human or vampires, should keep their mouths shut unless they were feeding or sucking cock. I was glad to hear that he'd no longer be poisoning the younger generation of new vampires with his Old World bullshit.

"That seems a bit stupid, considering the age of some vampires," Nathaniel interjected, oblivious to the import of Fáolán's words. "They could gainsay whatever the Council claimed."

"You might start taking notice of what vampires are meeting unfortunate endings, young one. Your Janos, my dear Siofra, was one of those who did not see eye to eye with their goals," Fáolán said coolly. "Simply your association is what puts you in their sights as well."

"Why would they even consider doing something like that?" Nathaniel gasped. "Who knows what those vampires might have accomplished? They're shooting themselves in the foot by doing that."

"It is all about control and very little to do with common sense. They wish to be the godhead of our little society, and are doing everything they can to eliminate any potential demigods who might stand in their path to success in that endeavor."

"Demigods?" I asked.

"They see anyone who might have a certain age and background to be a threat to their designs, real or imagined. You are a vampire without a kiss, well, unless you consider your offspring, here. The Council wants vampires who stick to the old ways, and not those who have discovered they are able to function without close supervision," he said. "That makes you a very real threat to their plans."

"Is that why you ended Orellos?"

"I ended him because he was near enough for me to do so. I might have faced my own end for doing it, had the Council not needed me as their personal recording device. While some might be sad to see Orellos sent on to the next life, they would have been far more concerned if I had been ended in his place."

"How did you end him?" Nathaniel wanted to know.

"I dismembered him. Slowly." Fáolán replied with a wistful look. "It took a long time for his end to come, and I enjoyed every last little bit of it. He'd been the one to bring me over in the first place."

So, the child had ended his parent. I should feel some sense of outrage for that, but knowing the what and the why of Fáolán's own turning, I couldn't muster it.

"He begged for a quick release near the end, but I refused. He wasn't ended until I finally took his head by twisting slowly around and around on his neck and his spinal cord finally snapped," Fáolán finished, a satisfied smile on his face. We were silent for a time before conversation resumed.

"Bravo, Fáolán," I told him, meaning it. "It sounds as though he deserved what you gave him."

We kept talking as we walked, and he shared with us exactly what the Council was bent on accomplishing. I was not particularly surprised at what he revealed to us, but the scope of their plan was ghastly.

They wanted a tight little community, but one built upon *their* rules. They had no problem taking out any vampire who did not see things their way, or who they believed would loudly question their views. Apparently, the latter reason was why I was being targeted.

I was shocked to hear that they had already arranged for and accomplished the end of at least two dozen older vampires, including Janos. His family was being sought as well, but as far as Fáolán knew, their location had not yet been discovered. For whatever reason, Janos had decided not to include me in that information, and now I'd never be able to ask him why. Perhaps he believed that I'd be safe, ensconced as I was in the Middle East with my fledgling.

"I'm sure that Janos had established at least a few good hidey-holes over the centuries. He would want his family to be safe in the event of impending disaster. I have an idea of where one of them is, at least. When I think its safe enough, I'll check there," I told him. "Estelle may have left me some kind of word in case I needed to get in touch."

Oh, I was sure she had. We had got on like a house afire once she knew I did not have my sights set on her Janos. She also knew that I would do whatever I could to keep her family safe, even at the expense of my own life. Estelle would do the same for me.

"You really think you can take on these others all by yourself," Fáolán scoffed. "They are too strong for you to be able to do such a thing."

"I won't be by myself. I'll have Nathaniel with me," I replied. "Between the two of us, we should at least be able to make some kind of a dent in them."

"A dent? You'd be lucky to scuff their surface!" Fáolán snorted. "Best you find yourself a hole to hide in and make as small a noise in the world as you are able."

"Pretty fatalistic, aren't you?" Nathaniel piped up, some disdain in his voice. He had better watch himself, or things might end badly for him. "Don't like what's going on, so you decide to end yourself, and then you don't have to watch it all happen, right?"

I guess I had been right about his tone of voice. Nathaniel never saw it coming, but I did.

Rather than saying anything in reply, Fáolán swung his arm sideways, his clenched fist connecting with Nathaniel's chest and knocking him at least a hundred feet away. Instead of waiting for Nathaniel to return to fight, the older vampire strode over to him and stood over him, fangs bared and eyes burning with anger. Fluid oozed from a small wound on Nathaniel's forehead and down toward one of his eyes, but he ignored it, his gaze locked on Fáolán's face.

"How dare you question me or my motives, infant!" the ancient one raged quietly. "You know nothing about what I have experienced since I became as you see me now! You are presumptuous and downright rude. Siofra has failed miserably if she has not taught you manners and respect for those older than yourself."

"She's taught me to have respect for those who are deserving of it," Nathaniel riposted, rising to his feet and dusting himself off. "You're taking the coward's way out, wanting to end yourself. If you were an honorable person, you'd help us fight to keep the Council from doing what they're trying to do."

Fáolán quite literally snarled at Nathaniel, his anger up and his previously amiable nature erased from view. I wondered if I was going to have to step in to keep something permanent from occurring that might piss me off and end up with me ended as well. I was surprised to find myself thinking about Nathaniel's welfare over my own.

He slapped Nathaniel across the face, knocking him back to the ground again. This time, Nathaniel came back up with a few more scratches on his face and arms. His manner was still defiant, however, and he stood right back up again to face Fáolán, who was still in no mood to listen.

"I've been the slave of the Council for scores upon scores of decades now, little one! Don't you dare accuse me of not doing my duty!" he grated, face to face with Nathaniel. "I'll tear your head off and leave your maker to bury what's left!"

"Really? You don't seem to want to get involved in much of anything," Nathaniel told him harshly. Why, oh why could not the boy realize it was time to leave well enough alone?

Once more, Nathaniel went flying, but this time, Fáolán just about moved as quickly as he did, and was right there when my offspring came to rest in the dirt. Blind fury suffused Fáolán's face, and I saw that he was on the verge of crossing a line I could not allow him to cross.

"I can't let you damage him further, Fáolán," I interjected. "I understand that you're mad at Nathaniel for what he's said, but he's right. You're planning to sneak off and end yourself and leave the Council to someone else. That's cowardly as hell."

The vampire whirled to face me, his fingers curled into talons, and his fangs looking like long ivory spikes to my eyes. I saw my ending in those eyes, but I had to give Nathaniel a chance to get the hell out of here while he could. I would do what I was able to distract Fáolán long enough to enable an escape.

"I don't want to see any of them again," he cried. "I've done my time and I deserve some happiness before I leave this plane of existence. If they capture me again, I don't know if I'll be able to escape again."

Fury, horror and despair filled his face and his voice. It was a terrible thing to see and hear, and I did not like strong-arming him into helping us, but I couldn't see that I had a choice.

"Fáolán, I know you hate them. I can't imagine what it was like to live the kind of existence you have, but you know them better than anyone else does now. If what you've said is any indication of your value to them, they've got to be out there looking for you," I said quietly. "You're a valuable commodity to them, and they literally cannot afford to let you slip away. We can use that as a tool to find them, maybe."

A flash of movement and I was abruptly thrown a few dozen yards from where I had been standing a moment earlier. Instead of following me just as quickly, he stalked to where I lay on my back and then stared down at me, fury in his eyes.

"This is like asking someone who has been burnt to put their hand back in the flames, Siofra. How can you do that to me?" He demanded. "Have you no compassion? No mercy?"

"I do, Fáolán. I really do," I replied. "And it will take a strong man to be able to put his hand back into those flames, Fáolán, but I think you're strong enough to be that man. That vampire."

Fáolán shuddered wordlessly, and I could almost feel the revulsion he felt at my suggestion. After what he had been through for so many centuries, I experienced some guilt at pressing him on this, but we really did need more help, so I continued to press my case.

"We have to put an end to these backward, megamaniacal bastards and send them on to the next life, whatever that may be. Nathaniel and I can't do it by ourselves. We just don't have the knowledge or the resources but with you doing your part, we stand at least a chance of succeeding." I pleaded with him. "Don't you want that?"

The fury had gone from his eyes but not the desperation. I could see the war going on inside of him: the part that wanted to obliterate the bastards, and the part that simply wanted to hide away and have nothing to do with any of it. I could only hope that he came to the decision I wanted.

"You know what they did to you because they discovered your gift and coveted it. What's to stop them from doing it to some other human? Would you wish this upon anyone else?" Nathaniel asked reasonably. "I think you're probably a better person than that."

Fáolán turned away for a short time, knuckling away the blood tears that had begun to brim and then turned to face me again. For a moment, I was afraid that he was going to throw me across the landscape once more, but instead he reached out a hand and curled his cool fingers around my own, pulling me back to my feet.

"Asking questions like that is what the Council fears," Fáolán said then. "They only care about vampires, and specifically themselves. In their eyes, no one else matters, especially not the humans, beyond their status as cattle. I believe that if they were able, they'd warehouse them all and not let them learn anything at all."

"Being compassionate should not be limited to our own kind, Fáolán. I came from a time when compassion for humans was unthinkable, and it took me at least two centuries before I began to have any compassion for them," I told him, brushing myself off. "I don't go overboard with it, but I know I wouldn't wish your own situation on one of them."

"Well, I don't like it, and everything inside of me is screaming at me to run in the other direction," he told me. "However, I will do what I can to help you both with this."

"Thank you!" I exclaimed, and put a hand on his shoulder, squeezing gently. "Every little bit helps."

"Save your thanks. I'm still not at all happy about this," he replied curtly. "If I am captured, I will do everything I can in order to end myself in that instant. I will not be their captive ever again."

We resumed walking in the general direction of the concealed car. I could hear some of the nocturnal wildlife as they emerged from their dens. Some would be looking for bugs and such, while others would be hunting those who hunted the bugs. It always made me glad that nothing ever cared to eat vampires. That is not to say I had not been attacked on occasion by something that apparently felt it needed to defend its territory, but that was the exception, rather than the rule.

Another quarter mile of silent walking and we finally reached the Mercedes, covered in its layer of dust and brush. He raised an eyebrow and looked at Nathaniel and then at me. I was gratified to see a glint of humor in his eyes.

"This is the chariot that will take us out of Iraq? I'm assuming you are headed for Jordan, am I correct?"

Chariot. Funny.

"Since I'm fairly certain they're keeping an eye on the airports, going through Jordan seemed the most reasonable way to get the hell out of here and then on to Europe. I have somewhere we can stay there," I said. "I haven't been there in several decades, so there's no reason they should think I'd go back there. If they even know about it, that is."

We clambered into the car and got going. There was a minor dustup when Nathaniel attempted to assert himself as "He Who Rides Shotgun", but Fáolán pulled rank and my offspring was left to sulk in the back seat. He pulled out his now somewhat battered laptop, plugging it into the power inverter we'd put into the car so he would not run the computer's battery down and listened to music through his headphones and read an e-book.

I smiled a little when I heard the faint stylings of Rammstein whispering out of the thing. My offspring was growing up. I had always liked whatever the "new" music was for any given time. That did not mean that I ended up disliking things as they were supplanted by new lyrics and melodies, but I tended to listen to the older stuff less and less. Well, opera has never been a favorite of mine. Tragedies have never been my thing.

"I was told yesterday that the border wait is currently about five hours long, Siofra," Fáolán advised me quietly. "It's a thankless wait and you'll have to maintain your composure while we do."

"I know," I replied. "I've had waits like this one in the past. Nathaniel has not, but he's a quick study. I think he'll be fine. We can only hope we aren't faced with someone who is particularly nosy."

I remembered the Gestapo officer who'd thought he would rape me in exchange for his stamp on my papers. The pig had escorted me off to an unused office and had me bent forward on the desk, my stockings down around my knees as he tried to take me from behind. He had screamed like a girl when I twisted in his grasp and ripped out the front of his throat with my fangs bathing in his blood, even as I drank it down.

He had stunk of cigar smoke, but his blood had been excellent. One less nosy Gestapo officer was always a good thing. That had been during my second trip to Germany during World War II when I had gone in order to help some friends make good their escape.

It did not take long until we saw the lights of some of the vehicles that would precede us into Jordan. Once we joined the queue, the truck in front of us turned off their engine. It would be our turn to alert the next vehicle to arrive, at which time we'd turn off our own engine and lights. It seemed a good system.

Fortunately, the drag on our fuel did not last too long, as we grew our tail about ten or fifteen minutes later. I was quiet, as Fáolán rested his eyes next to me, and I did not want him to have to take in any more stimulation and memories than was absolutely necessary. I had thought to give him my noise-cancelling headphones in order to mute as much outside noise as possible.

Nathaniel was still reading behind me. We'd never been much for random conversation, so that was fine, under the circumstances. He's seemed to understand what I was trying to do for Fáolán and was not rocking the boat.

Every five or ten minutes we'd move forward again. Most people in line seemed to wait until they had at least two car lengths of space in front of them before they turned on their engines to move forward again. There was no sense in wasting any more fuel than was necessary.

I only saw one instance where someone tried to cut the line. I really don't want to know what they did with the driver after they dragged him from his car and took him out into the desert. His screams suddenly cut short, and the self-appointed posse came back without him, dusting off the fronts of their clothes.

The system worked as long as people followed the rules. Don't follow the rules and those around you would get an idea of what lay in store for rule breakers.

Itinerant vendors walked the seemingly endless line of cars, hawking their wares. Overpriced snacks, bottles of water, and even souvenirs passed as we moved along. I was reminded of the Mexican border with the United States, and was almost disappointed to not see any clay donkeys or strawberry pots amongst the offerings.

We were about fifteen miles along in our snails' parade when we were approached by a furtive looking human with a curiously pale face.

I could hear his heart racing and when I sniffed the air, I could smell his fear.

"Good evening," he said nervously, stepping close and peering into our vehicle. "Are you headed into Jordan?"

Were we headed into Jordan? Why else would we be waiting in this ridiculously long line of vehicles? I kept my thoughts to myself, wondering what it was that he wanted.

"Yes, we are," I replied. Fáolán's eyes came open and he turned his head to stare at the interloper. His look was not friendly, which made me wonder what was going on. "Can I help you with something?"

The human's eyes widened as he saw Fáolán and I saw shocked recognition register there. His heartbeat rose to the point that it was almost a hum in his chest, and it appeared he had suddenly changed his mind about whatever it was he wanted from me. Whatever it was about Fáolán, he did not want to be anywhere near him. That much was obvious. He took a half step backward and made as if to turn away.

Before I could say anything further to the human, Fáolán reached across from his side and dragged him through the driver's side window, across my lap and into the front seat with us. He was not at all gentle about it. I smelled the stench of urine as the terrified human lost control of his bladder. I hoped it was not so much that he left a real mess behind.

"Hello, Eugene," Fáolán said to the human who now sat between us. The ancient vampire had pushed the baseball cap he'd worn to conceal his face back so that his eyes were now exposed. "Who sent you on this little quest? Do you still labor for the same master, or have you been passed along to a new master?"

"Eugene? How do you know him?" Nathaniel asked from the back seat.

"This one works for the Council," Fáolán said to no one in particular. "He's a spy, and he knows what happens to the Council's unsuccessful spies, at least, the ones who don't die when they're foolish enough to allow themselves to be discovered. I'll solve that problem for him right now. He won't have to face them and tell him of his failure."

"Please, master! Spare me and I will be your servant!" the desperate human cried out. Fáolán looked at him with disgust in his eyes. "Please don't kill me!"

Fáolán shook the human hard to shut him up, and I heard the popping of his spine as its alignment shifted from the force of the vampire's shaking.

I think Eugene would have cried out at least in protest of the rough treatment he received, but the human never had the chance. Fáolán had cut off the human's oxygen supply in the course of dragging him into the car, causing him to faint. I hoped the inhabitants of the cars in front of and behind us had not noticed our little drama, as I did not know how I would even begin to explain things.

"This one started working for the Council about fifteen years ago, shortly after I was captured after my last escape. Eugene hopes to be granted entrance to our peculiar society after a time of service," Fáolán explained as the human was rolled into the back seat to lie in a heap next to Nathaniel. "Only a fool would believe anything the Council promised them."

"Was he looking for you?" Nathaniel asked.

"I do not believe he expected to see me here. I think he was looking for you both," he replied. "I do not know if he would have had someone else here with him, but I would think it is no longer safe for us to stay in line. We will need to find an alternate way into Jordan."

Well, wasn't that just spiffy? The road would have been the easiest way to make our way out of Iraq, but I guess we were out of luck now. Damn the human's unexpected intrusion into our personal drama.

"What other ways are there out of here," I demanded. "The border wall is long as hell. I'm assuming they have measures in place to keep people from simply heading over it on their own."

"Indeed, it will not be easy, but it seems that we have no choice in the matter, unless you wish to remain here," Fáolán said. "In either case, the human must die, as he has seen all of us together, and I'm fairly certain you have no wish to free him, even with your vaunted compassion."

I ignored his dig and nodded, thinking hard on what we would need to do. After staying in the line so long, to end up having to move out of it and take another route wasn't high on my list, but I saw no other alternative now. The open desert wasn't necessarily going to be a friend to our escape.

"Consider our next move quickly, Siofra, as I see more movement coming this way," Fáolán urged. "I would imagine they are checking on the status of their former compatriot. It would be best that we are on our way quickly."

Cursing softly under my breath, I started the car and used the single car length I had created ahead of me to make the tight U-turn only a little bitty Mercedes like this could make and sped away down the highway, back the way we had come. Those who had been approaching must have been human, as I saw them fade away into the distance. That, at least, was a good thing. As far as I knew, they did not know where they had lost this human, and we could have been turning around and leaving for any number of reasons.

At least, I hoped that was the case.

"The wall is particularly tall," the ancient vampire said. "Perhaps even taller than we can top without extra equipment. There are also patrols and guard stations all along its length, as well as mines along the way."

"Mines?" Nathaniel interjected from the back seat. "Why the hell are there mines?"

"Yes, mines," Fáolán gave an ugly laugh. "If one is lucky enough to make it to the border fence, they still must try to make it past the explosives that have been so cunningly planted there to keep people from making their own border crossing."

I hated mines. I had lost part of one arm a few years ago when I had not quite been fast enough to escape the explosion of the mine that I had triggered as I ran over it. The shrapnel had done plenty of damage as well, by some miracle doing only minimal damage to my head. The bandit who'd been chasing me had not been so lucky, but he was killed before I was able to feed from him in order to heal myself. Running around one-armed, perforated and oozing ichor over several days before I found an opportunity to feed had not been fun in the least.

Continuing on the road was not a good idea, since there was a chance they'd seen what we were driving, or would find out from those who had seen us leave. I also knew that trying to off-road in the Mercedes would not end well for the little car, but covering as much ground as I could manage before the tires and wheels gave out was preferable to running it. I had no choice, and I knew it.

I turned the car so that it traveled in the dirt, keeping our headlights off and relying on my enhanced vision to keep me from having a close encounter of the bad kind as we left a dusty cloud in the air behind us. It would not be long until dawn arrived, and I wanted to be as deep into the desert as I possibly could before it did.

Seven

I won't bore you with the details of the trip to the border wall, except to say that by the time we got to within a short distance of the mine field that had been set to dissuade those who would have attempted to scale it, the poor Mercedes had lost its tires completely and was running on its rims. Yes, there had been some discussion of running the remainder of the way to the wall once the tires were no more, but ultimately, it was agreed that we should make use of the car as long as we were able.

The human was conscious once more, although he cowered in the back seat, knowing that his time was short. Perhaps he thought that if he remained quiet enough, we'd forget about him and let him live. If that was the case, then he was mistaken.

I stopped the car near a sign that warned of mines both in the Iraqi language and in English. We'd gone as far as we safely could with the car. Now we were left with only our feet to take us to relative freedom. I knew that our pursuers would still be looking for us, and might indeed be close behind. We did not have the luxury of time to consider our options.

"What are we going to do with the human," Nathaniel asked from the back seat. In the rearview mirror, I saw the human twitch in fear. "I'm surprised we've let him live this long."

"Oh, I have my plans for him, don't you worry about that," Fáolán purred from the front seat. He turned to look at the human who sat diagonally from him. "Eugene liked to tease me when I was chained to the wall and could not feed. He thought it was funny to watch me lunge against my bonds."

"I only did as the Masters decreed, my lord! I am innocent!" the human cried. Even I was unconvinced of his sincerity. Did humans not realize that a vampire could hear the beating of their hearts, which was a far better lie detector than the tone of one's voice.

"You and I both know that they never told you to torment me, Eugene. Fools they may be, but they would never have allowed you to do that to another of their kind. You always waited until they were gone before you began your one-sided game with me," he said. "Now that we don't have chains to separate us, I'd like to try playing your little game, myself."

I took in a breath through my nose and enjoyed the stench of fear that was flowing from the human in response to Fáolán's words. He knew that his end wouldn't be simple or anything approaching merciful. I wondered if Fáolán would let us watch, or if he would take the human somewhere he could exact his vengeance in private.

"When I would misbehave, the Council would decide that I would not be allowed to feed for a month or more. They would always make sure I fed before I lost my mind completely, but if you have ever been unable to feed for an extended period of time, you know what happens and how desperate you become. This one found my helplessness amusing," Fáolán told us. "I was the one vampire he could bully and as long as he was not caught doing it, he'd survive another day."

Fáolán smiled hungrily, licking his lips and showing off a bit of his fangs as he gave the human his complete attention. Eugene's end was near, very near.

Knowing that we should give him some privacy, I climbed out of the car and nodded at Nathaniel to do the same. The human in the back seat began to scream and beg, but the ancient vampire had no mercy in mind.

We watched from a distance as Fáolán reached over the seat, clamped a hand on the human's left upper arm and dragged him over the back of the seat and into the front seat. At first, the human tried to wrest his arm free of Fáolán's iron grip, but was unable to escape what would be his final encounter with the vampire.

Fáolán took the human's free hand in his own and regarded the pudgy fingers there. He raised the hand to his mouth and licked at the fingertips. I could see even from this distance that the human's fingernails were unusually clean. I was not prepared for what I saw next.

The vampire opened his mouth, sucked the human's right index finger into it, and then bit it off at its base. The human's scream was high and terrible, like the sound a rabbit makes when it's hurt.

Fáolán settled in to drink the blood that flowed from that wound, rather than drinking from the human's throat. It was evident that Fáolán wanted to make this last as long as he possibly was able. From what I had gleaned of their history together, the human had earned this awful ending.

As it was, Fáolán must have been drawing in deep swallows of the human's blood, as it was not long until the human started to become weak and sleepy from blood loss. At that point, the vampire was able to remove his hand from Eugene' upper arm and truly settle into the business at hand.

No, that was not a pun. I promise.

I was surprised when I saw Fáolán stop drinking long before he would have taken the human too far to survive the blood loss. He pushed Eugene over on the seat so that the human was on the driver's side, lying on his back, blinking lazily.

"Take him out of the car, Nathaniel. He's not done atoning for his actions just yet," Fáolán called to us. He spoke in an ugly voice. "He has one last service to perform for me, and I don't want to forget myself and take too much blood from him before he has completed his task."

Without a word, Nathaniel went and did as he was bid, bringing the human over to stand with Fáolán next to the warning sign. I moved to join them, our lone backpack slung over one shoulder, but holding all of our important information.

"So, then, what's the plan," I asked Fáolán. It was obvious that he had something in mind, but so far, he had not shared what they might be. "How are we going to get across the minefield with as little damage to ourselves as possible?"

"By this point, I've drunk enough of this fool's blood that he's not going to be too aware of where he's being pointed. I propose to aim him in the general direction of the wall and then send him on his way," was his answer. "He'll keep walking until he either reaches the wall, or he comes to an abrupt end. Either way, we can follow his footsteps to find the clearest route to the wall. With luck, he'll go a decent distance before things go all sideways for him.'

It was a coldblooded plan, but I could see where it made sense. While we were vampires, we were not really capable of easily ferreting out mines buried beneath the sand and debris that littered the area. That debris included human bones, so it was apparent that we were not the only ones who had attempted this crossing.

Fáolán was taking this time to gently slap the human on the cheeks to get him to rouse at least enough to be able to walk. He cajoled the human in a deceptively friendly voice, the human so out of his mind that he did not know how much danger he was in right now.

"Wake up, Eugene! The Masters want you! Run to them now," he cried, turning the human to face the minefield before us. He released Eugene and gave him a gentle shove on the back to send him on his way.

The human staggered forward, mumbling reassurances to his unseen masters that he was coming and would be there soon. I thought I caught something about his having something tell his masters, and that it was important. He clearly had no idea that he was fast approaching his own ending.

We watched as the human moved forward in a raggedly straight line toward the wall. He listed to the left and to the right every so often, but got a respectable thirty feet before he took a wrong step and we suddenly found ourselves being pelted with bits and pieces of human flesh, bone and blood.

The human in question, obviously mortally wounded but still alive, lay on the ground screaming in agony. It was funny how pain could bring someone to full alertness.

Eugene was missing one leg up to his hip, the grotesque wound looking like a badly cooked hamburger, with some bits blackened and others raw and bleeding. Knowing what I did of mine fields, I surmised that this one was peppered with AP mines that were more intended to seriously injure than to kill those who happened upon them. That was good information for us to have. We might make it through the field yet.

"We have at least another hundred feet to go," Nathaniel said. "How do you propose we clear that area?"

"We use the vehicle, young Nathaniel," Fáolán replied. "We will set it on the same course as Eugene took, and perhaps it will be able to travel even further before it also comes to its own end."

I had visions of pieces of a suddenly and violently dismantled Mercedes falling around us, and found I was not too keen on that idea at all.

"Where do you propose we stand to avoid becoming a casualty, then, Fáolán? One well-placed chunk of metal and one or more of us could find ourselves ended," I said. "I don't want to have come this far only to have myself ended by a well-aimed car part."

"Unless the vehicle rolls across a mine intended to take out other vehicles, we should be spared a hail of metal, rubber and assorted electronics. All we need do it make it to the top of the wall and we can run along that until we are sure we are able to land in a mine-free portion of the Jordan-side of the wall," he told me. "I would suspect that the anti-vehicle mines are much fewer and far between."

"I wish he'd just die already," Nathaniel muttered, waving vaguely at the human who was now making soft gurgling sounds as he bled out onto the ground.

"Well, he did manage to pull himself along another fifty feet or so before he stopped moving, Nathaniel," I said as I looked over and saw the human's amazing progress. "And at least it was in the right direction, more or less."

The human, who had not just lain where he was, waiting to die, had pulled himself with his arms and one remaining leg, further toward the wall. He had had enough presence of mind, perhaps, to crawl away from his tormentors, anyway. The human's path described a faint arc, and I was surprised how he had gotten to where he now was without locating another mine in the process. That one would probably have taken out Eugene's head entirely and ended his mapping of a safer route for us to travel.

Fáolán started the Mercedes and then moved it back from the warning sign by about twenty feet. He then aligned it as close to the path the now apparently deceased human had traveled to send it on its last errand. Slipping the little car into neutral but not shutting it off, he rolled down the driver's side window before he got out, then closed the door. After that, he stood a moment, eyes closed, with his hand on the roof.

I saw his lips moving, but heard nothing. A benediction, perhaps? When he opened his eyes, he slapped the Mercedes's roof in a chummy way and then turned to us, a smile on his face. The smile did not quite meet his eyes, so I knew he was far more apprehensive than he pretended to be.

"At least it's an automatic," he noted. "It would have been much more difficult to pull this off with a manual transmission."

With that, he leaned in the window just a little, slipped the car into drive, causing it to slowly start rolling forward under its own power. An automatic Mercedes of this age could move on what can only be called "impulse power" and get to about fifteen miles an hour. Thinking about it, I realized that would be a perfect speed for the car to travel, as anything faster might cause it to bypass a landmine or even veer out of control. That would make what we were trying for here meaningless.

When it got to and the passed the edge of the minefield, I could not take my eyes away from its progress. It managed to travel about three quarters of the total distance the human had before it started to veer off-course. There had not been a way to keep that from happening, so it was not unexpected, but I would have wished it had made it further along the way. Instead, it pulled a bit left, but kept on toward the wall.

If I had required oxygen, I would have been holding my breath as the Mercedes continued along on unexplored ground. About twenty feet later, a mine exploded beneath it, destroying the left rear tire, but not stopping its crawl much at all. Unbidden, I gave a quiet cheer at the car's mechanical tenacity.

The explosion sent it back toward the right a bit, and it managed another ten feet before it found another mine that must have taken out the gas tank. A flash of white and the Mercedes was engulfed in flames. There was an unexplored swath of ground about ten feet wide that we would need to bypass, but that was certainly much better than what we had originally faced as an obstacle.

I knew that the black oily smoke would soon attract attention, so we had to get moving, and quickly. Who knew if that attention would be friendly or unfriendly, and I really did not want to wait to find out which.

"Follow the tire tracks and run!" I yelled unnecessarily. Fáolán was already most of the way to where the car still burned, with Nathaniel not far behind him. I knew that Nathaniel was capable of leaping great distances, as it fit with his preferred method of hunting. My concern was whether or not we'd be looking at similar mines on the other side of the wall, and we wouldn't know that until we got a look from the top of the wall itself.

Fáolán covered the distance easily and leapt to the top of the wall almost in the same movement as his running, as though he were simply clearing an obstacle along the way instead of jumping to the top of a twenty foot wall. All in all, it was very impressive. Especially as the top of the wall was covered in razor wire. It was old and a bit rusty, but since tetanus was not something a vampire has to worry about, I was only concerned about accidental amputations of my fingers.

Nathaniel, on the other hand, had a little trouble with his leap and ended up hanging from the edge by the fingers of his left hand. I heard his snarl of frustration and felt a surge of anger as I saw Fáolán continuing to run away along the edge of the wall, not stopping to help.

Of course, the ancient vampire was not geared toward helping other vampires as a rule. I was sure it was out of character for him to have aided us as much as he had already. I, however, was not as single minded as he.

Gathering myself for my leap and crouching at the last possible moment to get enough power under me to clear the distance, I still was unable to land on my feet, and instead had to grab the edge of the wall with both hands and pull myself up to the top. It was a bit difficult to get my footing with the razor wire taking up the middle third of the wall, but somehow, I did manage it.

Once I got safely to my feet, I bent and grabbed Nathaniel's wrist to pull him up to the top of the wall. There was a sharp pain as one of the blades of razor wire cut into the skin of my calf, so I took a half-step forward to get away from it.

"Siofra, I'm losing my grip on the wall, and I can't swing my other hand up to grab the edge!"

"Grab my wrist and I'll try to get you up. There's razor-wire up here, and my balance isn't as good as it might be," I told him. "Try to move as carefully as possible. I've already sliced myself once on the stuff and don't want to do it again."

Wordlessly, Nathaniel wrapped the fingers of his other hand around my wrist and working together, got him up to safety. It took all the self-control I could manage to keep myself from stepping back to try to get a more sturdy footing, but somehow, we did it. A glance showed me that Fáolán was nearly out of eyeshot, so we'd have to hurry to catch up with him.

In the distance, I could see flashing lights approaching, and came to the conclusion that military authorities of some sort were coming to investigate the black smoke that billowed up from the quickly disintegrating vehicle. Standing around to find our bearings was not in the picture for now.

"It's not going to be easy, but run along the exposed edge of the wall," I said to him then. "Just keep an eye on your footing and keep putting one foot in front of the other, and do it as fast as you can."

With that, I started my own run along the wall, running more with the tips of my toes than the rest of my foot. I did not look back, trusting Nathaniel to keep up. We did not have the time to dawdle.

I was reassured to hear his steady footfalls behind me, and simply kept running.

Looking down on the Jordan side of the wall, I saw no evidence of land mines. Instead I saw a nest of tangled wire and what looks suspiciously like the remains of animals both recently and long dead. I had no desire to become a part of that particularly gruesome graveyard.

I was just able to make out what appeared to be a clear spot a couple hundred feet ahead of us. I was sure that Fáolán had taken that route to escape. The problem would be getting over the razor-wire that currently blocked our path. I saw no way to avoid being seriously injured by the blades on our way over. I would be very surprised if Fáolán had been unable to avoid hurting himself.

"Nathaniel! It's not much further," I yelled over my shoulder. "I see a hole in the fence line. It's going to hurt to get there, but at least will be the hell out of this country!"

"If I can spend less time looking over my shoulder, I'll be the happiest vampire in the world! Just let me know what I have to do," Nathaniel exclaimed.

"We're almost there," I reassured him. "We just have to figure out how to get over this fucking wire!"

"Why does that sound ominous, Siofra?" he wanted to know. "This shit is nasty!"

"I know it is, Nathaniel, but you're going to have to jump over the wire," I explained. "That's after you throw me over the top."

I should not been surprised that he did not voice objections to this. I knew him well enough by now to know that he would have done it without even having asked my opinion first. That was just the kind of person Nathaniel was, and I did like that about him.

A few moments later, we arrived at our destination. Nathaniel looked up and down at the curl of wire that split the countries of Iraq and Jordan. I could see a bit of apprehension in his eyes, but then I saw grim determination replace that and he looked down at me with an almost shy smile.

"Are you ready for your flying lesson, Ms. O'Se?" he asked. He bent and made a stirrup with his linked fingers. "Mount up!"

I slipped my foot into his hands and in one movement, he lifted me and hurled me over the deadly wire to land on the soil of Jordan.

Eight

While my arrival in Jordan was mostly painless, Nathaniel was not so lucky. In order to protect his hands as much as possible, he had removed his *keffiyeh* and wrapped it around his right hand. In the act of vaulting the razor-wire, his left hand emerged fairly well shredded while his right hand sustained little damage. The profanity this engendered ran the gamut of English to classic Latin. I knew that the Greek and Italian words he used had been learned from me during our years together, I could only assume he had learned Latin while he was still human.

"I don't care who the first human is we encounter," he told me. "I refuse to walk around looking like I stuck it in a garbage disposal. You could do with a quick feed yourself."

He pointed down at my legs, and I followed his gaze to find that my calf, which I had thought only barely cut, was in fact deeply sliced. It must have been the sheer desperation that had kept me from noticing how bad it really was. Nathaniel was right. I needed to feed soon, or the open wound might attract more unwanted attention.

"It's probably not a good idea to hang around here any longer than we need to," I said. "this area is probably mostly populated by military and government types. The humans tend to notice when those kinds of personnel go missing."

Nathaniel grumbled, but wrapped the remains of his *keffiyeh* around his left hand and off we went. I was glad that vampires aren't prone to normal bleeding, so the ooze that was coming from his shredded hand would remain hidden for a very long time. Perhaps even until he was able to feed and he could rid himself entirely of the thing, which was preferable.

"We need to find Fáolán, Nathaniel," I said. "I don't know how far away he's gotten, but it's important that he's still a part of this thing."

"The bastard literally left me hanging, Siofra!" Nathaniel retorted angrily. "I don't think we can rely on him to have our backs in this."

He had a point, but I really did not want to do this without more help. While my first thoughts after the death of Janos had involved visions of my taking out all of them on my own, I had had enough time to consider things to know that there was no way I could do that. These vampires were a part of the Council because they were sly bastards who could probably talk or think their way out of anything. It's not as though I was indestructible, after all.

I was about to answer him when a shadow caught my attention and I looked up to see Fáolán gesturing at me from the dark side of what was probably an equipment shed. It was plain to see that he wanted us to come over to him, so I took Nathaniel's relatively undamaged right hand and complied.

"Honestly, I'm surprised to even see you again," I told him. "You ran away so quickly that I ended up losing sight of you."

"We're going to be honest here?" He asked me. "Well, then, yes, I nearly did keep running. Then I remembered that I made a promise to you both and decided to wait for you both. I don't like it, but I'll stay to help. I won't risk myself, but I'll do what I can."

"Risk yourself?" Nathaniel asked him. "I thought you wanted to end yourself."

"No, by risk myself, I mean that I won't put myself in the position of being captured again. I'll tell you now that if it looks as though that may happen, I'm gone. You'll be left to your own devices, because I will never be taken again!" He replied.

"At least we know that now," I said. "I know that we may not be able to rely on you in a fight, so we'll deal with that. I'd rather you were all in, but frankly, we don't have the numbers to pick and choose. I'll take you as you are, with your preconditions."

He nodded and began to start off. I grabbed his arm to stop him.

"But know this, Fáolán. If you do something that causes Nathaniel to be caught or worse, ended, I won't give you the opportunity to run. I'll chain you to a wall myself." I ground out at him. "I'll keep you from feeding and watch as you descend into madness. I promise you that."

Looking as though he meant to say something, Fáolán looked into my eyes and must have seen something in there he did not like and kept silent. Considering that he was over six feet tall and I a mere five foot two, it was odd to think that I might have intimidated him. It did not bother me, but it *did* give me something to think about.

We slipped out of the border town as quickly as we were able, and simply ran until we found a place we could rest for the hot daylight hours. We were becoming dehydrated and as we did not know when we would feed next, conserving our bodies' moisture was paramount.

I had been keeping my eyes open for some kind of rocky outcropping, but Fáolán instead directed us to a thick patch of brush it appeared as though it had not seen water since the Great Flood. I was amazed it had not turned to dust and blown away long ago. A large portion of Jordan was simply desert, and rain in this area was infrequent at best.

"We can hide ourselves deep within that," he said. "It will be safer for us to travel at night. If anyone from the other side got suspicious and contacted someone on the side of the border the last place they're going to look for us is under something like that."

"We need to get to Ar Ruwayshid as soon as possible. Our contact is meeting us there, and I haven't had the time to find another cell phone to contact her to let her know our numbers have increased," I told Fáolán. "I don't think she'll get too pissed off at the surprise, but it's never nice to surprise people like that."

I had not mentioned the arrangements to Nathaniel before this, our relationship allowing him to trust me to make the right decisions without question. He gave me a glance at my words and nodded acceptance. Fáolán, on the other hand, reacted as I expected he might. I understood his paranoia, but he really should try to get over it.

"Contact? How nice it would have been if you had shared that information with me earlier," Fáolán said, giving me a dirty look. "I believe I have been more than accommodating coming along with the two of you. Why would I want to include another in what to me is already a very uncomfortable situation?"

"Sasha isn't a threat to you, Fáolán. She hardly deals with any other vampires, at least in the time I've known her. You're safe with her," I replied. "She's the one who has the jet that will get us the hell out of here and back to Europe."

"She has a jet and has nothing to do with the Council?" he asked me, his face showing how much he doubted it. "If she has that kind of money, she would be a natural for the Council."

"She doesn't have much use for authority of any kind, Fáolán. If she did not value her privacy so much, Sasha would probably have told them to go screw themselves long ago. Hell, she may have already have done so, as until the other day, I had not even spoken to her in at least the past thirty years."

"Thirty years, and she is still willing to help you? That seems unlikely to me," he retorted. "Perhaps she has changed in that time."

I gave him my own dirty look and raised an eyebrow at him.

"You're just determined to find any reason at all to duck out on this, aren't you? I knew Sasha's maker before he made her. He was murdered by duplicitous humans a couple hundred years ago. As for the Council, she has always stayed as far away from them as she could manage."

"I do not know a 'Sasha'. Who was her maker? I am sure I would have heard her name mentioned at some time during my captivity," he asked.

"Sasha isn't her real name. She changed it about twenty years after he made her vampire," I told him. "She did not like her human name and decided to choose one she liked more. Even Sasha is a name she came up with after the first time she changed her name. As she doesn't care to be bothered, she's probably changed it at least five times over the years. The Council may not even be aware that she still exists."

"Hmm," he replied, a thoughtful expression on his face. "I suppose you won't share with me the name of her sire."

"It is not my name to share, Fáolán. If you ask her, and she desires to share it with you, that is up to her," I told him. "I'll let you broach the subject. I won't get involved in that."

This time, Fáolán stayed quiet and led us into the thick dead brush, where we rested until nightfall. None of us spoke before we slept. It was hot, and even a vampire may be rendered lethargic in the heat of the day, as when we are unable to stay in cooler areas, our bodies lose their moisture more quickly than is normal.

While we had fed from the humans who had kept us captive the previous night, I was already beginning to feel hunger pangs due to the extreme heat and stress we'd experienced over the past twenty-four hours. I hoped we'd be able to take care of that before we met Sasha, but knew that was not very realistic of me. It was going to be one very long run to Ar Ruwayshid, and we'd likely all be in bad shape once we arrived.

I hoped Sasha would be able to help with that, because I tended to get more than a little grumpy when I started down this particular path.

Nine

I was not paying a lot of attention, buried as I was in the middle of the thick brush, but through my doze, I would hear periodic foot traffic passing within mere feet of where we concealed ourselves. Jordanian soldiers had clearly been sent to look for whomever had managed to breach the wall, but thankfully, none of them thought to look in our wildly improbably hideaway. Our naturally cool body temperatures kept us from showing up on heat-sensitive equipment as well, so there would be little reason for anyone to go looking there in the first place.

We lay still until it was full-dark out, and I was reassured that there was little foot traffic in the area. Inhaling deeply, I could smell the faint scent of human. I doubted there was a human within thirty yards of where we were hiding. I looked over to Fáolán and Nathaniel and saw their eyes were open, and filled with a sense of waiting and anticipation. We all seemed to know it was time to go.

"I don't think we have time to slip out of here, so we should probably just run for it. Even if someone does hear something, we move fast enough that I doubt anyone would even think a human had been responsible for the noise they heard." I suggested. "You ready to go?"

I was in really worried about Fáolán, he could always be trusted to look out for himself. Nathaniel was my one concern. He gave me a short nod, and I saw him begin to gather himself to leap off and run for it. Trusting him to keep up, I stood up and bolted, running as fast as I possibly could, never looking back. Fáolán was up and away faster than I could track, and I could hear the sound of Nathaniel's pounding footfalls behind me as he strove to catch up with me. Further behind me, I heard some kind of interrogatory sound I presumed to have come from one of the humans near where we had hidden, but it never rose to the level of an outcry.

"Keep running west, Nathaniel," I called, loud enough, I hoped, for him to hear me. "Ar Ruwayshid should be large enough for us to see some illumination from artificial lighting there!"

"We haven't run like this in a while, Siofra," he responded. "You know this is going to take a lot out of us!"

"I know, kid!" I replied, slowing enough that we were now running neck and neck, making it easier to talk without having to yell. "Just do the best you can."

"Fáolán sure disappeared fast enough," he commented, nodding into the empty distance. "You think he'll stop in Ar Ruwayshid?"

"He wants to get the hell out of here and can't trust many other vampires. I think he'll take a chance and at least hang around long enough to be certain he's not falling into unfriendly hands," I said. "Well, that and he's going to want to feed as soon as he can. Even though he's an ancient, he can't avoid the inevitable."

"Who is this person who's helping us out?" He wanted to know. "Why haven't you said anything about them before?"

"I've known Sasha for a very long time. Her maker was one of those who did not like to be bothered. He had a group of humans who were content to feed him in exchange for their personal safety, so he felt no need to become involved in the affairs of our community. I only met him because we encountered one another the first time I met Janos on one of our forays into our community's unique form of justice."

"Oh?"

"Yes. I received the message that I had to meet this unknown vampire in Nancy, which is in France. At the time, I was on the far side of Germany, and had only about a week's time to make the trip. I bought a fast horse and tack from a livery stable and then was on my way."

"A horse? Could not you take a train?"

"There were not widespread passenger trains until a few years after all of this happened. A carriage would have drawn too much attention, and I was not in a position to run the whole way, either. I nearly killed the first horse by just about running it into the ground. I was easier on the two horses that followed that one. You don't get much trade-in value on a horse that's nearly done in."

"But how did you meet Francesco during all of this?"

"I knew the horse would drop soon, so I slowed a bit to keep him from dropping in his tracks and then started looking for a likely livery stable where I might find its replacement. While I was unsuccessful at finding what I wanted, I did find Francesco's manor and its pastures."

"You did not just steal a horse and keep going? That's unlike you," Nathaniel said. "Why do something different?"

"These were purebred warmbloods in the pasture, and all were branded with the mark of his stable. I did not need to worry about people keeping their eyes open for a horse thief, so I knocked on his door and introduced myself."

"So right off the bat, he opened the door and you found yourself facing another vampire? That seems odd to me."

"No, it was a time when the master or mistress was very rarely the one who answered the door. His footman answered the door and I was ushered in, after introducing myself. A stable boy rushed up to grab my spent mount's reins and led him off to Francesco's stables, I assumed."

I remembered the meeting very well, even now. It had turned in to a pleasant surprise, all around.

I was bid to wait in the library, where I spent a good twenty minutes looking at the titles on the spines of the hundreds of books I found there. Whoever lived in this place was very well read, and the volumes very well kept. A monstrous atlas sat atop a wide table, its pages open to a rough map of the New World. I wondered what this person's interest in that mysterious continent could be, and then finally perched on a dainty horsehair couch that abutted a coffee table strewn with knickknacks and gewgaws.

When the massive door to the library opened again, I stood and faced what appeared to be an elderly human male. His eyes widened a bit and he quickly turned to close the door behind him, taking a small key from his pocket and locking the doors behind him.

"*Nosferatu?*" he blurted in shock. He swept forward and took my hand in his, kissing the back of it quite formally. "It has been many years since last I laid eyes upon one of my own kind! I am called Francesco."

Yes, I faced another vampire. Genuine shock glowed on his face, and he gently pressed me back down onto the couch, sitting beside me, still holding my hand in his. I could not tell how old he was, but it was evident that he was at least a few hundred years old. He spoke German, but it was evident that it was not his natal language. It was clear that he had lived quite a full life before being turned, as his head was crowned with a full crop of thick silver hair. He had not been clean-shaved when he was made vampire, as his chin sported a neat van dyke-style beard.

"I am surprised beyond all measure to find another Nosferatu here, myself," I replied in the same language. "I thought I was familiar with those who were so well established. I am called Siofra."

He laughed delightedly, patting my hand, which he still had not relinquished.

"You are an unfamiliar sight to me, as well, young lady," he bubbled. "I see by your name and your accent that you are Irish. May I be so bold as to inquire as to your own history?"

Vampire manners. While it was considered rude to ask an older vampire about their origins, it was considered to be good manners to be forthcoming if the question was asked to you by one older than you. I was pleased when he slipped into Irish Gaelic, which I had not spoken in quite some time. I had missed its musical tones so very much.

"My sire was called Andreas," I told him simply, also in the Gaelic. "I know little of him, as my own turning was accidental. Once he found me after I awoke, it was too late for him to make the bond."

"Andreas made an accidental vampire? Oh, that's just delightful! I always knew he was so self-centered that he wouldn't notice the obvious, even if it bit him." he laughed again. I rather liked his laugh. "I'm assuming that you fought him tooth and nail while he fed from you, and that is why you rose as the vampire you are now?"

I nodded wordlessly, and he dissolved into even more laughter.

"Surely that is something that has happened more than a few times in our kind's history. One would hope that most have not been left to their own devices thereafter." The old man observed. "Andreas is an ass, and you were fortunate that he did not have the raising of you. He holds tight to whatever he has, possession and offspring included. Had you made that bond, I doubt you would be out alone even now."

It was obvious that he was quite familiar with my maker, so I did not elaborate. I would let this vampire make his own suppositions.

"What brings you to me today? I'm sure you had a reason for doing what you did to that poor animal upon which you rode."

I told him that I was on a vitally important errand, and that I wished to purchase one of his fine animals for the journey. At this, his expression become cross and he dropped my hand as though it had burned him.

"As I said only a moment ago, I have seen what you have done to the poor animal that you rode here. I could not in good conscience allow you to do that to another. While I may keep myself separate from the majority of humanity, I have always loved my horses."

"I have had a horse for most of my time as a vampire," I told him. "I left my last horse behind when I removed from Scotland to Dresden. She is now happily cropping up grass in an enormous pasture that she shares with a few cows and an irritable goose."

We argued and haggled a bit before he finally allowed me to take one of his animals, on the promise that I would

"And that went well for him for quite some time, until one of the humans on his lands decided that he or she wanted money more than security, and Francesco was ended. Sasha had been on her own for decades, and since no one really knew much about her, the first she learned of his ending was when she came for a visit and found the mansion burnt to the ground and the grounds ransacked."

"When was this?"

"About 1840 or so, which was maybe twenty years after her sire's murder? She slaughtered the small band of humans she found squatting on the property and then made arrangements to have the land kept wild and permanently guarded. As I recall, the terms of the Trust she created state that no new humans may ever live upon the land."

"New humans? How has she managed to keep the land from being taken over by someone else, or even the government, itself?"

"At this time, there are no humans residents on that land. Instead, it is inhabited by a clan of Leone who migrated there shortly after World War II," I said. "They needed a safe place to live and raise their cubs, and this gave them that opportunity. They raise enough livestock and feed to make enough money to pay for their own upkeep, and Sasha's inheritance continues to pay for the land's taxes. While Sasha had originally intended for the land to remain uninhabited, she realized after the War that leaving it completely alone would only encourage squatters and possible government interference. She welcomed the Leone when I brought them to her attention."

"How did you find out about all of this," he wanted to know.

"Sasha and I met again in Sweden about five years after that. I was visiting with one of Janos' offspring, and she was running wild as only a vampire could in those days. With things being so very unsettled at that time, it was not that difficult to make one or more deaths look relatively innocent," I told him. "She fed off an entire family of humans who had had the audacity to steal from her before escaping to England. They were under the mistaken impression that no one would know what they had done."

"A whole family?" Nathaniel stared at me, shocked.

"Almost every single one of them. At the last, she decided to spare the children, deciding they should not have to pay for the transgressions of their parents. I've known some vampires who would have slaughtered the children as well, done to the youngest babe," I could see a glow in the distance. "It appears as though we're nearly there, Nathaniel. We're almost out of here."

We managed to avoid encountering any groups of humans, but left the lone ones alone for now. It wouldn't help to be strangers in town and suddenly people started going missing. The authorities always seem to start their questioning with people they don't recognize and I would rather not have that kind of attention directed at me at any time. Nathaniel and I had decided to feed just before we left the town and to not leave anything behind that might inspire anyone to put two and two together and arrive at ourselves.

We found Fáolán sitting at a rickety round table outside what must have been an all-night café, pretending to sip a coffee and looking around with a bored expression on his face. The only light came by way of a pair of heat lamps, keeping his face mostly in shadow, but he was not too difficult to recognize.

Fáolán beckoned to us to join him, which we did, and he waved over the server and ordered coffees for us as well. I saw that his own cup was half-empty, and wondered what he had done with the half that was missing, as vampires cannot ingest anything but blood. The ground beneath him was dry, so I was at a loss.

Then I saw a brown wad of what appeared to be tissue clenched in one hand and realized that he was spitting the brown fluid into that, probably under the guise of being fastidious and wiping his mouth. I had done something similar a few times over the centuries when there was not a potted plant handy to accept my own offerings.

"Where are you supposed to meet this friend of yours, dear lady," he asked me. I assumed he avoided using a name for me in order to maintain our anonymity. "I don't believe you mentioned that when last we spoke."

"She knows me by sight and scent, and will be looking for us already. I'd described my friend here to her as well. You will be the only surprise from me on her list today," I told him. "Just be patient and we can just keep ordering here, I suppose. Wandering around would just make it harder for her to find us."

"I have some false papers on my person," he volunteered. "Will she be able to use those to help me leave here as well?"

"She's pretty efficient and creative, so I have faith that she'll be able to help you out as well," I reassured him. I saw him tapping the fingers of the hand that held the coffee-soaked tissues on his leg, but ignored it. "If she doesn't find us by dawn, I'd be disappointed in her, and that's rarely the case where she is concerned."

Fáolán was more than likely one of those constantly nervous people who always expected the worst. That way, they aren't disappointed when things just don't go their way, and when this do go well, they can be pleasantly surprised. I tended to be more of an optimist about things, since I had found that if I set my mind to getting something done, I would usually succeed at it.

The server came back with two tiny cups of coffee that balanced atop two wildly mismatched saucers. I smiled at him and put out my hand to take my coffee from him, as Nathaniel did the same for his own. He asked if we'd like a little biscotti, I nodded my thanks, and the server disappeared back into his shop, where I could hear him rummaging around.

"Doesn't say much, does he?" Nathaniel commented. Fáolán turned to him and snorted.

"You can imagine that I appreciate that more than he could possibly know," he replied. "I told him that I was waiting on friends and that we might sit and chat all the night long, if that was alright with him. At the sight of the rather large handful of coin I gave him, he allowed that he was willing to remain all night long to refill my cup, if that was my desire."

The elderly server returned with a plate heaped with the hard little black and white toasts and a small pile of napkins, and then returned to the depths of his shop. As we were his only customers at this late hour, and appeared content to sip and nibble, he probably wouldn't return until we actually required his presence. From what I gathered, Fáolán had already paid the man handsomely, so he was not worried about us taking a proverbial five finger discount.

Once I could hear that he was busy elsewhere, I took two of the biscotti from the pile and slipped them into one of my pockets. I decided I could throw them away when we left. It made more sense for us to pretend to eat the things. Nathaniel followed suit, while Fáolán ignored them entirely.

"I used to eat these things all the time," Nathaniel said as he slipped the hard bread into his pocket. "I loved them, and now I have no desire for them at all."

"There's something about what we are that makes those cravings disappear," Fáolán responded. "I always enjoyed the sweeties I'd snatch from the candy-maker, and would keep a small stash of them whenever I could. Once I became as I am now, that sweet tooth disappeared entirely."

"There is something to be said for that," I said. "Imagine spending the rest of your existence seeing and smelling things that you craved and could no longer consume. Not something fun to consider."

Nathaniel shuddered and picked up his coffee cup from the table, pretending to sip at the stuff. He reached over his free hand and squeezed my thigh.

"I'll be happy when we can be somewhere that we don't elicit suspicion just because of our appearance," he sighed. "That's been the worst part of all this for me, I think."

"This is true," I agreed. "However, you have an easier time here than I could ever have, considering my bright red hair."

He laughed and ruffled his hand through my hair.

"Well, it's lovely and you certainly have a lot of it," he replied. "I don't think mine is anywhere near as impressive as yours."

"I know a few of our kind who were balding, but not bald, when they joined the family," I told Nathaniel. "Imagine spending your life like that."

"I guess it's good that I had a full head of hair, then," he responded. "I'm rather fond of what I have."

"I know. I've seen how much time you spend on it whenever you have the chance," I . "laughed. "It looked so very odd that time you had to shave it all off."

We'd been searching for a now-dead human monstrosity known as "Death", and we'd had to disguise ourselves more than once on our quest to locate him. Since he could regrow his hair at his next feeding, he had shaved off all of his hair and gone into the town we were scouting to ask questions. To establish "who" he was, he had taken off his keffiyeh at one point, exposing his naked scalp. That was the feature the villagers would remember above all else if and when anyone talked about it. He would be an entirely different person to them if they saw him again once again sporting a thick head of hair.

"It felt odd," he told me. "I really don't want to have to do that again unless it's absolutely necessary."

"Really? I know some of us who do shave their heads daily, as they prefer the easier upkeep it offers them," Fáolán interjected. "I've done it myself, on occasion."

"Do it with my blessing," Nathaniel replied. "Bald just isn't me."

"My recently departed friend kept his head that way for about fifteen or twenty years," I told Nathaniel. "He was traveling through areas that did not offer many amenities, and he was always fastidious about his appearance. He would take a straight razor to his scalp as soon as he'd eaten and keep it close shaven enough that you'd think there had not been anything there for a very long time."

"Where was he traveling?" Nathaniel asked.

"Through the American colonies," I said. "He was tasked with establishing Havens in the original colonies, and I believe he did not want to take any of their parasites along with him as he went from place to place. Lice and fleas were very common in those days, even in the cities. Herbal hair colognes were invented as a way to discourage their attaching themselves to one's hair."

"He was a stronger man than I, then," Nathaniel opined. "I'm too used to what I have up on top."

My attention was taken by a shadow that approached from a corner diagonally from where we sat. As my vision sharpened, I realized that it was a local policeman, and he was making a bee-line for us. He saw me looking at him and waved a hand at me, a slight smile crossing his face as he walked.

"It is unusual to see persons out this late in the evening," the policeman said in good English. His head of thick black hair was uncovered, but clipped close his scalp. "Might I ask what you are doing here? I don't recognize you."

"We are waiting on a friend," I told him truthfully. "I'm not sure when she's going to arrive. We're not in any hurry, so I thought it would be nice to sit and chat while having a coffee."

The officer considered that and then nodded to himself.

"What is this friend's name," he asked reasonably. "Perhaps I am familiar with her."

"Her name is Jennifer Tate," I replied. "We haven't seen each other in many years, and when we found out that we'd both be traveling in Jordan on holiday, we decided to meet here."

Two thirds of that was the truth, anyway.

"I have not seen or heard of this person," he told me. "At least, not until just now."

"She may still be driving," I said. "She prefers driving at night, when it's cooler out."

"So you plan to simply sit here and wait until she arrives?"

"That seems to be the way of it," I laughed, smiling at him. "Could I interest you in a cup of coffee?"

The officer seemed surprised, but pulled a chair over from the table next to us and sat down, introducing himself as Zaid. The server, as if by magic, appeared at Fáolán's elbow to take a new order.

"Where are you from?" he asked us once his coffee arrived and he had doctored it to his taste. "You are obviously not Jordanian."

"Scott and I are from the States, and Jules is from Ireland, I think," I responded, using the names that agreed with the papers we now held. "It's Ireland, right?"

"Close enough," Fáolán replied. "It's been a very long time since last I was there, however."

"I'm surprised that you wouldn't stay in one of the larger cities. This place isn't much, tourist-attraction wise," Zaid allowed. "Wouldn't you like to see the more civilized part of my country?"

"I like to see the real country," I told him. "I like seeing the real people and culture. Not something that's been carefully manicured for the benefit of tourists. Don't you like doing things like that, yourself, Zaid?"

"True," he replied. "I supposed that if I visited your country, though, I'd want to see the big cities such as New York and Los Angeles, and maybe even Chicago. Are there small towns you would recommend, if I did go there?"

"It really depends on what you like to see and the season," Nathaniel interjected. "If you went, do you know what time of year you'd want to go?"

"Probably the summertime," he said. "I would like to go somewhere that did not get too warm. What would you say to that?"

This felt like an examination of some kind, but I played along. I squeezed Nathaniel's leg beneath the table to keep him from talking, which was something we'd done many times over the years.

"In the summertime, I'd stay away from a place like New York, unless you don't mind humidity. Actually, New York isn't much fun in the winter, either. It gets bitingly cold," I told him. "But that's the big city. For a smaller place in the summer, I'd look at the small towns in Southern California. The west coast is peppered with them, both above and below Los Angeles."

This seemed to put him at ease, which made me wonder what he had been looking for in a suspicious answer. There was not a way I could broach that subject without raising those suspicions once more, so I was left wondering.

He chatted with us for about another fifteen minutes before he finally rose and excused himself.

"As much as I have enjoyed our chat, I must continue on my rounds," he said, real regret in his voice. "I wish you a fine time with your friend once she arrives."

"Thank you, Zaid! Please, take some of these biscotti with you on your rounds. A snack is always good when you spend so much time on your feet."

He thanked us all, giving a funny little bow to each of us in turn, and then strode off into the night once more. Fáolán gave me a strange look, but kept his mouth shut until Zaid was well away.

"Why did you invite him to sit with us and chat," he asked. "That was dangerous."

"It would have been far more dangerous to not be friendly and forthcoming. I've had to sit through waits like this in the past, and being friendly has so far not turned out badly for me during those times," I told him. "He was asking odd questions, so I know he's looking for something, but whatever it is, it's not us."

"He'll remember you more now because of the coffee and biscotti, you know," he said crossly. "It would have been better for him to forget about us entirely."

"Actually, he'll remember the nice friendly coffee and biscuits he had with the American tourists and their Irish friend one night," I countered. "We three were relaxed and composed, rather than nervous. We fit the stereotype of the average American quite well, as far as this country is concerned."

"Stereotype?" Fáolán nearly squeaked.

"We all know that people in this part of the world aren't very fond of outsiders, especially Americans. They haven't had much reason to trust us over the past couple hundred years, really. In their minds, Americans are either spies or loud, boisterous fools. In this case, I'd rather play the latter than the former," I said, speaking as quietly as I could. I did not want the shop owner to hear what I had to say. "Right now, I'd rather be dismissed as a fool than thought of as someone who must be watched closely."

Fáolán seemed to think this over and appeared lost in thought. While he might be at least a thousand years old, in some things, he was childlike.

The server came out came out a few times over the ensuing hours to freshen our coffees and provide even more biscotti. I could see how tired he was, and suggested that he take a nap for a time, reassuring him that we'd wake him when we needed either more coffee or biscotti.

"I could not do that!" he cried. "I would be a poor host if I abandoned you."

Great. A thoughtful overtired shopkeeper. Just what we really did not need. I had been surreptitiously pouring my coffee into a fat crack in the sidewalk, but the soil beneath would only hold so much liquid before it began to run across the cement. I wondered how many insects I had drowned when I had opened the caffeinated floodgates.

No matter how much Nathaniel and I entreated him to take some rest, the shopkeeper stubbornly refused to do so. The human appeared to be a very proud man who took his business and hospitality seriously, a trait more common with older generations than the current one.

"Would it be too much to ask that you make us three sandwiches to take with us, once our friend arrives?" Nathaniel asked him. "We won't be staying long after she gets here."

The shopkeeper brightened and nodded enthusiastically. He clearly was looking for things to do.

"What kind of sandwiches would you like?" he ventured. "We have nothing containing pork, of course."

"What do you recommend," Nathaniel asked, smiling warmly with that expression that would set a psychopath at ease. "What is your favorite?"

"I can make you eggplant sandwiches. Do you like eggplant?"

I'd never had the stuff while I lived, but nodded enthusiastically anyway.

"Eggplant would be fine," Nathaniel replied. "Once they're made, please wrap them up for us."

"They will take a little time, as I must cook the eggplant, first, but if you have the time, I am sure you will enjoy them," he assured us. "I have never had any complaints."

Humming happily to himself, the human went back into his shop and I heard a door open and close as he made his way into his kitchen to start making our order. With luck, it would keep him occupied for the better part of a half hour, at least.

"I hope this friend of yours arrives soon," Fáolán said archly. "We cannot remain here forever."

"I doubt we'll be waiting much longer," I replied. "She's never been one to dawdle at all."

We sat quietly for twenty minutes, enjoying the silence. Fáolán appeared to be thinking hard about something, while Nathaniel simply stared into the darkness. I wondered about Sasha. What she had been up to since last I saw her, where she was now, and how all of this would end.

Noble quest it might be, but realistically, we were three vampires pitting ourselves against at least one Council member who likely had a sizeable fortune he or she could afford to spend on keeping us at bay. That Council member would also probably have at four hundred years of surviving under his or her belt, so they would be prone to making few mistakes. It would be stupid to even entertain the notion that a Council member was acting alone. I knew enough about them to know that they all had their particular factions amongst themselves.

About forty-five minutes later, the shopkeeper arrived with our sandwiches, each wrapped in cling film and then tucked into a soft off-white cloth bag. He made sure we knew he had included a bottle of water for each one of us as well. I was actually beginning to feel guilty that the things would go to waste.

I was worried that we'd have to distract him with something else when I saw a familiar silhouette appeared on a nearby wall. If I still breathed, I would have given a sigh of relief.

It was Sasha. All four foot eight inches of her. She looked from me to Nathaniel and then rested her eyes on Fáolán. I saw recognition pass between them.

"I haven't seen you in a hundred years, old man," she said gruffly. "Glad to see you're out again."

"Felice?" he appeared shocked. "I thought you were ended long ago!"

"Hardly, old man," she laughed an ugly laugh. "I just went into hiding. I hold no more love for the Council and its minions than you."

"You two know one another?" To say I was surprised would have been an understatement.

"We've met a few times over the years, but I knew her as Felice," Fáolán told us. "I thought her long ago ended, the Council thinks her so as well."

"That was my plan," the vampire I knew as Sasha said as she dropped into the chair the policeman had once used. "I keep to myself. Imagine my surprise when I heard from this one here."

She nodded in my direction, never taking her eyes from the ancient vampire.

"So I'm assuming that you need a way out as well," she said to him. "You're lucky I have enough cold, hard cash with me to get you a stamp in your passport and a ticket to get the hell out of here."

"Thank you so very much, Sasha," I replied. I would only use Felice if she invited me to do so. "They murdered Janos a few days ago and there was not any way I could fly out of Iraq. They've got their spies all over the place. I'm only glad they did not know about Nathaniel."

"Indeed you are. If they had, they'd have sent more than—-four—-was it, assassins after you," she said. "Eight, at least. They know you well enough to know what you can do. That's why they used to send you on your own little errands."

"They stopped doing that about a hundred years ago or so," I told her. "Maybe they decided they could no longer trust me that time."

"Perhaps," she agreed, standing and leaning against the back of her chair . "Now, have you paid for your food and drink so we can leave without a fuss?"

"Long ago," Fáolán said, also rising. "Let us be off. I have had enough of the wind and sand for now."

I left a small wad of bills under my own cup, getting up as Nathaniel, ever the gentleman, pulled out my chair from behind. It was time to leave, and I could not get out fast enough.

"My car is a few miles from here. We can run there and then drive to the airstrip where my plane is parked."

"Our mutual friend here said something about your having your own plane," he said to Sasha. "I am unaccustomed to any but the Council having the kind of money necessary to afford the upkeep on something like that."

"I have quite a lot of money, my friend," she told him. "Enough that the Council really wants to have access to it, which is one of the reasons I was on their list in the first place."

"If they wanted your money and could not get to it, wouldn't they think you were still alive?" Nathaniel asked her. She laughed.

"I have my fortune tied up in so many ways, they can't get their bloodstained hands on it, no matter what they do," she chortled. "They went so far as to kill my former lawyer, but not before killing his wife and two of this three children in an attempt to make him talk. Even when he did talk, they killed him anyway, after they ended the one living child who remained. He did not know that the Council wouldn't let a human know about them and continue to live."

Her glee disturbed me a bit, but I said nothing. It was not my place to criticize her actions, as I'd practiced my own revenge on those who crossed me over the centuries.

Pot? Kettle?

Black.

So we were just about to start running when I saw a child's shadow nearby. He or she had a thin blanket pulled over their head in either an attempt to stave off the cold, or simple concealment. Bony fingers attached to a thin hand clasped the tattered edge of the blanket to pull it shut.

Grabbing the bag of sandwiches and bottles of water, I walked over and deposited it in front of the lump of cloth and flesh, not saying a word. Then I walked away just as silently, but not before I saw the fingers loosen their death grip on the cloth and move to pull the bag and its contents into the concealing folds of the blanket.

Nathaniel looked at me as I rejoined him, a question in his eyes.

"Too thin to make a meal of," I told him shortly, and began my run toward freedom.

Ten

Sasha's plane was really a small Lear jet, retrofitted to make it a comfortable mobile living space. When you live the kind of existence she has, being able to get the hell out of whatever mess you've gotten into as quickly as possible is generally the best way to do things.

As soon as she closed the jet's door, she demanded we hand over our passports and went to a small built-in desk, where she pulled out what looked like an old wooden puzzle box. After doing something to the box that I was unable to make out, she opened the lid and pulled out what looked like a stamp of some sort.

She grabbed a piece of scratch paper and stamped it a couple times with the device. Whatever it was seemed to have satisfied her, as she nodded and then stamped our three passports.

"This says you made legal entry to Jordan about two weeks ago. The stamp is good enough that it should stand up to reasonable inspection by German Customs and Immigration," she said. "I have a couple empty athletic bags that you can use to pretend to have luggage. Otherwise, they might look askance at your arrival."

"If they're empty—"

"I have some things you can sort through and shove in them to take up space. With only a few exceptions, I don't really feel a need to hold onto things," she explained. "We'll have to fake it for the old man, here, though. I had not made plans out that far for an additional refugee, but I think we'll be able to make do."

After pouring a small amount of sand into them all and then roughing them up a bit before pouring the sand out again, Sasha handed us back our bogus passports. Looking at Nathaniel's and my own, I saw that each held a slightly imperfect entry stamp purporting to have come from Jordan.

"Thanks, Sasha. I gather you're an old hand at this," I told her. "How many of those stamps do you own?"

"I have a half dozen of them and some other handy little tools in my box here," she said as she closed it back up again and tucked it back in its spacious drawer. "I'm sure you can understand why I don't use a regular lock and key setup."

Yes, I could. The box was ornate and looked more like a decoration than anything else. Unless someone knew what they were looking at, they'd ignore it. Since customs occasionally likes to make sure that jets aren't carrying contraband, keeping things as innocuous as possible in appearance was the order of the day.

I expected to see a pilot, and was surprised when Sasha was the one who climbed into that luminary's seat. She gestured for me to sit beside her, even as she told Nathaniel and Fáolán to sit and make themselves comfortable in the passenger section. I should not have been surprised that she had learned to pilot an aircraft. Sasha had never been one to sit and allow others to do things for her when she could do them herself. She had always been the very model of self-sufficiency.

"Get some rest, you two. I imagine you won't get much for a long time after we land," she called back to them. "There's a little something in the aft compartment, if you're interested, by the way!"

I heard a familiar sigh as Nathaniel rose and made his way aft, and then the sound of a door being unlatched. The aroma of overheated human filled the cabin and I was suddenly standing, and staring down the aisle at a storage area containing at least three bound and gagged humans.

"If I'd known we'd have another passenger, I'd have picked up another one before I left London," I heard her say faintly, as all I could really hear now was the terrified beating of three human hearts. "I can wait until we land. You all help yourselves!"

I could not have stopped myself if I had tried, I was dehydrated enough that I was almost on automatic. Sasha taxied down the runway and took off so smoothly that I barely even knew we'd left the ground and were now soaring through the air. There was not even that almost obligatory final bump as the wheels left the tarmac.

Nathaniel was already drinking greedily, the human from whom he fed too affected by heat exhaustion to put up much of a fight. I grabbed blindly and dragged out a fat female, her eyes already rolled back into her head and near death. I sank my fangs into the vein that throbbed at the side of her neck and drank down all I could from her unresisting body. My myriad tiny wounds and hurts disappeared as my body made thrifty use of the human's overheated blood.

Fáolán remained in his seat and watched us silently, every so often looking at the human who remained in the storage area, but reviving under the beneficial effects of the cabin's air conditioning. The fear in the human's eyes grew as he watched what was happening right in front of him, and he became aware of the fact that this would soon be his own fate.

I stopped my drinking shortly before my victim expired, and found Nathaniel looking at me, having already finished his own feeding. I could hear Sasha laughing from where she sat in the pilots' cabin, clearly pleased with herself.

"I haven't gone anywhere without at least a snack on hand ever since I got my pilot's license," she yelled back at us. "I learned my lesson on that while I was still a groundhog, and Havens were no longer safe for me."

"What do you want us to do with the leftovers?" I asked her. "We can't just leave them here, stinking up the place."

"I have some very large bags in that cabinet to your left, Siofra. You can use those to clean up," she said helpfully. "Put the bodies back in the storage cabinet once they're bagged up. I'll take care of them when we're in a safe place again."

I did as I was bid, folding the human into the fetal position before stuffing him into the thick black plastic bag Nathaniel handed me. Pushing out all the air I could from the bag with Nathaniel's kind assistance, I tied it shut tightly, if only to keep the stink of feces, urine and decomposition out of the cabin's air system. Then I helped Nathaniel with his own leftovers, pulling the single living human out of the cabinet before jamming the corpses inside.

"I'd prefer it if you ate over that plastic sheeting, Fáolán," Sasha piped up from the front cabin. "It makes things so much easier to clean up if you make a mess."

Fáolán pulled himself out of his chair and walked down the narrow aisle toward the remaining human. He considered the man and then reached out a hand to haul him up by one forearm.

"Where did you pick these up, anyway?" He asked Sasha.

"They were from a prison in Romania," she replied. "No, not prisoners. Guards. I decided to be nice and set the prisoners free before I took the ones who guarded them."

"You set criminals free?" Fáolán sounded aghast. "That was irresponsible of you in the extreme!"

"I did not say I set criminals free. I set political prisoners free. If they'd been criminals, I'd have left them to die, I can assure you of that," she told him. "I *do* have some standards, old man, no matter what you may think of me."

"Political prisoners?"

"Just because the communists are no longer large and in charge in Romania, it doesn't mean that some of the old guard isn't still there, trying to pull the levers of government," she chided him. "I turned loose humans who have been a thorn in the sides of the people who miss the old ways. Who miss Ceaușescu and his nightmare of a government? I'd like to think the ones I set free will take a little time to visit those who imprisoned them."

"Our little Sasha," I said quietly as I sat down again beside her. "Always thinking of the little things that make our world a better place. Ever the gracious hostess!"

"And don't you forget that, you Irish will o' the wisp! You had not spoken to me in a long time and then suddenly you call me, begging for help. That's a fine way to renew an acquaintance!" she blustered at me. "I don't know *why* I even came to your rescue!"

I refrained from reminding her of why her rescue of us was something she could not have turned down. She owed me and owed me big, and I knew she had not forgotten that debt in the least. It would have been bad manners to say something anyway, since she had accepted my call and come this far already.

"Somewhere in this flying yacht, you wouldn't have something like a washroom where I could clean up a bit, would you?" I asked her.

"Of course there is, Siofra!' she laughed at me. "I'm a civilized vampire, as you well know. It's just past the door to the left of the storage room you so recently visited. Make yourself at home. We've got about eighteen hundred miles to go before we land."

"Thanks!" I said and nearly bolted out of my seat and down to the washroom.

Opening the door, I gasped at the opulence of what could only be called a "washroom" if you wanted to be insulting.

A very high sided bathtub adorned one wall, with what appeared to be a clothes closet along the opposite wall, with a decent sized basin in between. As vampires do not relieve themselves as humans do, there had been no need to include a toilet, so there was none present.

I stripped off my clothing and let it fall to the ground, then climbed into the tub and turned on the water, gratified that it became comfortably hot almost instantly. Sitting down, I let the water rise to the height of my breasts before I turned it off and set myself to scrubbing the sand off of my skin and out of my hair. I found a nail brush hanging from a piece of colorful string over the tub's faucet and used it to clean the filth out from under my finger and toenails.

All in all, I spent perhaps a half hour soaking in the tub and working the dirt and sand from my body. It was a whole different kind of heaven. Looking at the pile of dirty clothing on the floor, I let loose a vile epithet as I realized I would have to climb into them once again.

I stood reluctantly as I pulled the plug from the tub's drain and watched the filthy water drain away. I imagined that it rained from some outlet on the jet's exterior to fall on whatever was several thousand feet below, but that was not my problem. I was now clean.

Gingerly poking at toe at the heap of filthy clothing, I was about to pull them on again when Sasha's voice came over the bathroom's intercom.

"And for god's sake, woman! Don't put those nasty ass clothes of yours back on. There's a loose sun dress I the closet you can use! Throw the dirty ones into the trash bin under the sink and I'll take care of them."

Walking over to the closet and opening it, I saw a collection of clothing that ranged from dresses to shirts, blouses and trousers. Quickly locating the sun dress she must have meant, something that did not clash too badly with my red hair, I pulled it over my head and returned, barefooted, to the pilot's cabin. I had grabbed a wide toothed comb from a drawer in the bathroom and was now pulling it gently through my hair to remove the tangles. I would worry about braiding it later.

"Did you enjoy yourself, Siofra?" she asked me, an impish smile on her wide mouth. "You looked as though you needed it."

"Needed it?" I replied. "I don't think I've needed a bath so much in decades!"

"Glad you enjoyed it, then," she replied. "Make sure you send the others back there, too. There's plenty of water to go around, as long as no one gets ridiculous, anyway."

I got up for a moment and popped my head into the passenger cabin.

"Nathaniel, get your ass in there and get cleaned up. When you're done, look in the closet and see if there's anything in there that might fit," I said. I did not bother to say anything to Fáolán. He was a big boy and not my responsibility. "It's not what you'll expect when you open the door."

Instead of going back to the pilot's cabin, I took the seat opposite Fáolán and looked at him. I could see from his color that he had fed, so that was taken care of, which was fine. Now it was just us vampires, which is what I preferred.

"Are you at least a little more comfortable, now that you know who Sasha is, Fáolán?" I asked him. "She's not an unknown quantity, and you know she has no love for the Council."

"Yes, I am familiar with Felice, Siofra. I was there when the Council decreed she had to be ended, as they coveted her fortune and thought that by ending her, they could just step in and take it all," he told me. "They were livid when they discovered that she had tied it in a financial Gordian Knot they were unable to unravel. All their plans of acquisition staked out in the sun to burn."

"She told me something about that. So you knew what they had planned?" I looked out the window, noting that for now, at least, Sasha was keeping us up above the clouds.

"Of course I did. I was generally kept chained or caged, if not both, in the main Council chamber. At one point, someone decided it would be amusing if they put a perch in the cage, as I was their parrot to learn and remember everything they ever said," his words came out in something that was almost a snarl, and I looked into his eyes to see blood tears brimming atop his bottom lid. "I was barely more than a clever animal to them, and I hate them for it."

"What better reason, then, to help Nathaniel and me wipe the bastards out," I told him. "Hell, it might even be a bit cathartic."

Fáolán scrubbed at the tears that threatened to fall with the back of his hand and gave me a tentative smile. It was probably the first genuine smile I had seen cross his lips since we'd met.

"You almost make me believe we can accomplish this, Siofra," he told me then. "You've the gods' own luck to you, you know. Any other vampire would have been ended by now."

"I have no idea what you mean, Fáolán. I was just encouraged to stick by something if I wanted to accomplish it, and so that's what I'm doing now," I demurred. "If whatever gods that may or may not exist choose to lend a hand, I'm not going to decline, but I think that only good investigation and then some hard fighting is going to bring any of this to a close."

"You've got a lot planned, Siofra, but be realistic now—" he interjected.

"Whoever this bastard is, he killed the first best friend I ever had," I almost shouted at him. "If I had not had Nathaniel to bring me back to sanity, I probably would have snapped and simply become a revenant when Janos was murdered. I can't back down now. I have to follow through."

Nathaniel walked out of the washroom with clean, though dripping, hair, barefoot like I was, but clothed in a pair of slightly oversized black athletic pants and a similarly over-large blue t-shirt emblazoned with the phrase "Hey, y'all, watch this..." with the image of a spilled can of beer beneath it. I wondered how much he had heard of Fáolán's and my conversation.

"I'll do whatever Siofra tells me to do, Fáolán, and it's more than simply because she's my maker. I only ever got to speak to Janos over the phone, but he was family to us both. You know as well as either of us how hard it is when you no longer can be near your human family. If you're a decent sort, you'll love them too much to stay around and maybe end up hurting them," he said. "So you're stuck either being a loner, which Siofra was until the night she turned me, or joining the family we've created between ourselves. You'd understand better if you had your own offspring, but from what you've told us already, I don't think you're ever going to do that."

"I cannot imagine doing something like this to another being," Fáolán said softly. "I just don't understand it one bit."

"Siofra found me dying, and for whatever reason, she decided to turn me shortly before I would have died," Nathaniel told him. "I'm not mad or in any way resentful about what she did, either. I would have passed from this world and that would have been that, except that Siofra helped me to survive, albeit in a completely different way. I was not ready to die at all."

"Are you really sure about that, Nathaniel? Would you have known any better if you'd simply left this plane to go wherever souls do after they've passed beyond the Veil?" Fáolán challenged him. "How can you justify feeding off humans in order to survive? Doesn't that make you a murderer?"

"There was a time when I felt as you did, but over time, I realized that a vampire is just another part of Nature who helps to thin the human herd," Nathaniel suggested. "Nature doesn't really care who dies. The strong and the lucky survive, while others die. It helps to keep things more in balance than they might be otherwise."

"I don't see Nature that way, young Nathaniel," the ancient one responded.

"Look, Fáolán. Humans are adept at surviving. Perhaps vampires were Nature's way of getting past those clever human defenses," Nathaniel told him. "When you can't get at them through disease or disaster, perhaps something as cunning as a vampire is needed to get through a human's clever set of defenses. I don't know if that's the case. I'm just throwing all of this out there, but it's an idea, anyway."

"You certainly are full of wild ideas," Fáolán snorted. "Does any of this actually have a point?"

"You can be such a cheerful person sometimes Fáolán, did you know that?" I interjected, almost shouting at him in exasperation. "Why must you always be so negative?"

Fáolán appeared to think about what I just said, though I could not tell from his expression what those thoughts might be. Maybe it had become hardwired into him to just be a negative son of a bitch, so at this point he just could not help it. All in all, it was becoming a real pain in the ass to deal with him, but for now I had no alternative.

"Maybe I should just keep my mouth shut then. Would that make you happier?"

I did not even bother to reply. I just hoped the moody bastard would hurry up and take his damned bath. Anything to get him out of my sight for a while.

"There appears to be plenty of hot water left," Nathaniel offered. "Might as well take advantage of it while we have the opportunity."

"A bath would not be unwelcome," he conceded, rising. "Please excuse me while I leave the desert behind. I pray you excuse my previous negativity, and will forgive a very old man who has become set in his ways."

I reclined my seat as far back as it would go, and closed my eyes. I planned to get as much sleep as I possibly could between now and when we landed. Who knew when we would have the opportunity to get more than catnaps once we were again on the ground?

Just before I drifted off to sleep, I suddenly wondered if Fáolán could somehow have read my mind. It was almost as though he had responded to my unvoiced thoughts.

I woke to Nathaniel's touch on my shoulder, and opened my eyes to see him looking at me with concern on his face. Looking around, I saw that Fáolán appeared to be sleeping.

"What's up?" I asked Nathaniel.

"You've been sleeping for the past couple hours and Sasha—Felice—whatever her name is, wanted you up front. I think she may be getting tired," he told me quietly.

I rose and wandered up to the pilot's cabin, plopping myself down in the empty co-pilot's seat. Sasha bestowed a welcoming smile on me and nodded her thanks to Nathaniel, who hovered behind me. I motioned for him to move back to his seat in the passenger cabin, which he did without a word.

"It's boring up here, and as sterling as your boy here's conversation may be, how about you regale me with the tale of your sojourn in the Middle East? We've got plenty of time for you to do it, too," she told me. "Another two hours or so, anyway."

I considered her words and how much I was really comfortable sharing. I decided I could share an abridged version of things. I would rather not bring any attention to our part in shaping the religious and political climate of a certain part of Iraq. I trusted Sasha, but there was no need to share absolutely everything.

So I told her of my turning of Nathaniel and our subsequent removal to the Middle East, where I could raise him under the best circumstances possible.

"I spent some time talking with him while you were snoring," she told me with a grin. "He seems to be a good kid. Polite, smart and funny. You got lucky."

"I suppose so," I said. "I turned him without knowing anything about him, first. On top of that, he's my only offspring, ever."

"I'm surprised. I'd have thought you'd have made another vampire long ago. Why did you wait so long?"

"You're one to talk. Have you made any yet?"

"Actually, I did have one, but she could not hack it and ended herself about twenty years ago." She replied softly, her eyes losing their shine and filling with grief. "I tried to talk her out of it, but she refused to listen. She left me a note while I was gone to feed one night, saying that she had chosen to end herself, and how sorry she was to have disappointed me. I never laid eyes on her again."

I knew this was about more than a vampire and her offspring. I got the very clear feeling that there had been something much more between the two of them, but I was not going to ask if this unknown offspring had also been her lover. Actually, I don't think that I even *needed* to ask that. I simply knew.

"What was her name?"

"Maude," she murmured. "She had amber eyes and beautiful thick, silky hair that went to her ankles. She reminded me a bit of the Leone with those lovely eyes."

"Where did she come from?"

"Scotland."

"Lovely country," I replied. "I've spent a few decades over there in total, I think."

"I just can't believe she chose to end herself," Sasha said sadly.

"I'm so very sorry, Sasha," I said. "I've known several vampires over the centuries who had similar things happen with their own offspring. I can't imagine it ever gets easier."

"What would you do if...?" she lets her words trail off.

"It scares the hell out of me," I answered. "So far, he appears to like, and even enjoy what he is now. When I found him, he was dying because of something stupid. It was not as though he was dying after some noble escapade or something along those lines."

We sat quietly for a while, absorbed in our own thoughts, but enjoying the companionship our proximity offered. I knew that her own maker had lost at least one turn in the years before he brought Sasha over, and that he had been reluctant to do it again. That is, until he had found a certain tiny fifteen year old girl who had been badly beaten for refusing to submit to the brothel owner to whom she had been sold.

I knew that Francesco had been a child prostitute in a brothel at some point during his time as a human before escaping from its walls, so something like this had a strong effect on him. Until the day he was ended, the one kind of human he absolutely refused to feed upon was a child.

When he saw that she had been damaged so much that she would die even with medical intervention, he had given her the choice of being brought over or not. Perhaps he had felt reluctant to turn someone who did not make that choice for herself and thus wanted reassurance that this was what was desired. I can only imagine what that conversation must have sounded like.

I lost track of time, but was brought back to myself at a guttural sound from Sasha.

"Maybe I'll decide to make another child in the future," she said to me with forced brusqueness. "For now, though, I'll keep to myself. At least until this bullshit with the Council and their minions is resolved."

"Does that mean you're coming along to help?"

"Siofra, none of us is safe until the old guard is ended and reasonable, modern vampires are elected in their place," Sasha said. "People, whether they are vampires, humans or Leone, need to be flexible enough to change with the times, and right now, that's not the case where the Council is concerned. So I'll help you with this as much as I'm able."

A smile crossed my lips. An honest smile. After dealing with the mercurial Fáolán, it was a breath of fresh air to have Sasha's open willingness to be of help. Maybe the ancient vampire would learn something about altruism from her.

Maybe that was wishful thinking on my part.

"How long until we land," I asked. "It's what, something like a four hour flight, correct?"

"Ya, in that neighborhood. It all depends on tailwinds and things like that," she confirmed. "We've been in the air for about three hours, so it won't be too much longer. I did not file a flight plan, so wherever we land, it's going to be a bit of a surprise for the local authorities."

"I did not think that filing a flight plan was mandatory," Nathaniel said, leaving his seat and coming forward. "Or is that just in the States?"

"It's not, but they tend to get their panties in a bit of a twist when you don't," Sasha replied. "Some airports are a bit more anal about it than others, especially when they're dealing with foreigners, Americans in particular."

"Ah, yes," I nodded wryly. "And they've caught on to the whole 'I'm Canadian', thing, too. If you're from anywhere in North America, there's every chance they'll think you're a possible spy."

"So what are we supposed to do then, if they get upset?" Nathaniel wanted to know.

"Leave it to me. I've got some rainy day cash set aside for the easing of paperwork. Can't make any guarantees that I'll be successful, but it's always worth trying, right?" She smiled. "Nathaniel, why don't you go and fill up those athletic bags with whatever you think would be appropriate travel items for the two of you."

I glanced at Nathaniel and nodded for him to do what she suggested. It was not as though we had to actually use or wear whatever he stuffed into the bags.

"Thanks again, Sasha. Or should I call you Felice?"

She laughed.

"Felice. Until today, no one had called me by that name since my centennial," she mused. "You might as well. It will keep the confusion down. Keep in mind, though, that the name on my papers is Valerie Upton."

"Valerie Upton. Okay, I'll remember that and I'll mention it to Nathaniel as well," I told her. "Where did you come up with that one?"

"The first name is something I pulled out of a book of baby names and the last name...well...it was inspired by a television program I used to watch. I've taken to changing my name and back story every ten years or so now. Too much electronic surveillance to

"Television? Really?" I scoffed. "Don't you have more important things to do than stare at the babble box?"

She laughed again.

"It's not all just stupid network television anymore, and a lot of it is available over the internet on demand," she told me. "You aren't stuck having to sit down in front of the television to watch it!"

"I know that, Felice," I retorted. "It's just that there are so many other things you could be doing with your time than watching visual pap."

"Pap? You've obviously never been addicted to a television program," she shook her head.

"Before I left the States, I ran my own company and did not have time to watch television," I said. "I had too many things to take care of to waste what little free time I had, and then Nathaniel came into my life and we've been away from most American television for around a decade."

"Most American television? What was there to watch?" she asked curiously.

"'Lucy' and 'Magnum' reruns, mostly," I told her. "Not my thing at all, really. As far as I've been able to tell, there is very little that is substantive on the air."

"Not all television is insipid trash anymore, Siofra," she said seriously. "There are now some programs on that are actually designed to make you think, rather than simply sweep you into another world for a half hour or more."

"I'll worry about that if and when we make it through this," I replied. "It's not the most important thing on my list to accomplish right now."

I settled into silence, continuing to look out the window, and enjoying the non-desert landscape I beheld below me as we made our way over the European continent. I did not know I could miss trees as much as I had during Nathaniel's and my time away from modern civilization.

Felice appeared to take my rebuke in stride and said no more on the subject. I have never been able to understand people who live and breathe television and movies when there are so many other things that can be done and experienced in the world. The babble box has nearly always been a waste of time to me, unless there was something in the news that was particularly important and the television could provide more information than the internet.

I was glad that Nathaniel had not been a television addict before I turned him. It would have driven me crazy to have someone constantly nattering on about something about which I was completely uninterested. It surprised me that Felice, as old as she was, appeared to be fixated on the thing, herself.

Before I knew it, I realized that Felice had the jet making its descent, and I moved to the passenger cabin to be sure that Nathaniel had us all packed up and ready for our disembarkation. I crossed my fingers that the Customs and Immigration folks wouldn't be too terribly upset at our arrival. I had ended government officials in the past, but these days, it was a lot more difficult to do so without creating a fuss.

I did not say anything else to Felice until I saw that she had flown over the big international airport and was heading to what appeared to be a less populated area. What the hell was going on here?

"I thought we were going to land at the main airport. What's going on now?"

"Thinking about it, I realized that it would probably be better for us to land on my property. I have a private airfield there, and with Leone there to keep out nosy humans, we can keep your arrival much quieter. Keep your passports with you, of course, in the event that you are stopped and asked for your papers, but I doubt that will be a concern," she replied.

"Wouldn't it have made sense for you to have planned this from the beginning?"

"Yes, it probably would have, but until now, I was not sure if I wanted you all the way out here," she said. "Anyhow, strap in and prepare to land. The runway is paved, but it's still a little rough on takeoffs and landings."

I strapped myself in and watched as we came in lower and lower, and Felice finally set us down on a spartan runway bordered by heavy forest. I saw humanoid figures melting into the trees as we landed, and knew that the Leone would be coming back soon to make certain the new arrivals were allowed to be there. The only question was whether they would arrive in human form or in their natural feline shapes.

The landing was mostly uneventful, barring the roughness of our touchdown. Glancing back to where Nathaniel and Fáolán sat, I could see my offspring's eyes locked on the landscape outside the window and knew he had likely missed thick forests at least as much as I had. Fáolán was his usual enigmatic self. While he stared out the window, his face remained unreadable. I was unable to determine if he was happy or unhappy about his return to Europe, but I was equally confident that it wouldn't be long until I found out, whether I wished to or not.

As the jet taxied to a stop at a shack that could only be called terminal if one was being facetious, Nathaniel, Fáolán and I rose and made our way toward the door. I looked forward to smelling air that did not reek of the desert, a desire that truly surprised me. I was rarely this anticipatory.

"The Leone will probably be on us soon," I told them both. "I saw them going into the forest as we touched down, but they won't be gone for long. How familiar are you with them, Fáolán?"

"I haven't seen the Leone in several hundred years. I had thought them extinct until fairly recently," he replied. "Roman and Greek hunts for so-called 'European lions' were actually a pogrom instituted against them. The last Leone about whom I knew was slaughtered in a cave in what would later become Armenia."

"I found out about them in the late 1930's," I told him. "I helped them to escape Germany before the Second World War truly got under way. The clan I was able to assist was part of a larger group that is also in the part of the world we just left. Some of their descendants are probably still here on Felice's land."

"Really?" He glanced at our savior with something resembling at least a small amount of respect. "She did that?"

"I sent them her way when they needed a safe haven from the Nazis," I said. "She gave them a home and the Leone had some interesting hunting when unexpected and unwanted guests would arrive to loot the ruins. I'd say it worked out pretty well for everyone concerned."

I could see Fáolán turning all this information around in his head as I related it to him. He had been such a loner for such a very long time that it was not part of his personality to help others in need. He had had to look out for himself for at least five score centuries, and had only been able to trust himself during that time.

At least, I assumed that was the case, judging by his actions during the past couple days.

Once Felice opened the jet's door, we were out and down onto the tarmac. Shortly thereafter, forms both human and feline slipped out of the forest and slowly approached us. We stood perfectly still, allowing them to identify us for what we were so they would know we were not a threat to them or their cubs.

"Hello, Hans!" Felice called as she swung out of the jet and leapt to the ground. "How have things been since the last time I visited?"

A muscular, tawny Leone bounded up and shifted back to human form right in front of her. Long scars ran down his chest, and Felice reached out a hand to trace the worst of them, not saying a word. I had seen Leone do this when they showed off their own scars to other Leone visitors. They were a mark of accomplishment and something to be proud of amongst them.

Hans the Leone stood quietly as she did so, unselfconsciously naked, a slight breeze moving his dirty blond shoulder-length hair gently. The vampire suddenly lurched forward and enfolded the Leone in a strong bear-hug, which the Leone, not always quite so physically demonstrative, tolerated in good humor.

"What in the world did that to you, Hans?" she asked him, leaning back again to stare at the scars on his chest once more. "Is it still alive?"

The Leone laughed, gently pushing her away and taking up the sarong one of the human-shaped Leone handed him, expertly wrapping it around his waist and tying it in a tight knot at his hip. I had never known a Leone to be self-conscious about nudity, but perhaps things were different with this clan.

"Some government flunky came by, looking to survey the property. The transit he was using did this to me," Hans replied in Old High German, which gave me an idea of how long this group of Leone had been isolated from society in general. "I fed it to *him* before I fed him to my mate and cubs."

"Did anyone come by looking to see what had happened to him," Felice asked, switching to Old High German, herself. "I was not aware they were trying to make free with my estate once again. I'll have to check into that when I have the opportunity. They really should know better than that by now."

"There were two or three petty functionaries who came by to check on him, but they did not stay long. We'd moved his vehicle several miles away, along with all his equipment," he told her. "And you know how expert we Leone are at cleaning up after ourselves. It's the only way we've managed to survive this long. I'm thinking they decided that he'd run off, taking a couple thousand marks' work of equipment with him."

"And no one came back to take over where he'd left off?"

"We've done our best to give the property an eerie feel ever since. No one seems to want to complete the job," he chuckled.

"It's not even their property to fiddle about with," Felice snorted. "And they know it. Hans, keep an eye on what they're doing, please. I think they may try to take bits and pieces of my land a small amount at a time. Make sure that fence line doesn't somehow end up changing."

"Of course, my lady," Hans promised her.

Throughout this discussion, Fáolán had been staring at all the Leone around him, his eyes wide and filled with wonder. He had told me he thought the species long dead, and now he had empirical evidence of their continued survival.

He dropped to his knees as a Leone cub came sniffing up to his feet. Carefully and cautiously reaching out a hand, he caressed the dome of her skull. When she did not protest, he slipped his fingers under her chin and gave her a good scratching there. A deep, rumbling purr rumbled out that brought a smile to Fáolán's lips.

"Hilda is in the middle of her first year," Hans supplied helpfully. "I'm sure she likes the attention."

"She's lovely," Fáolán breathed appreciatively. "I haven't laid eyes on one of your kind for at least the past several centuries. I was surprised and very pleased to hear of your survival to the present day."

"We don't get many visitors who don't end up on the dinner table, so to speak," Hans chuckled. "Why don't you all come and spend a little time with the clan before you leave again? We have nothing appropriate for your own needs, but conversation is always welcome."

And with that, we found ourselves, hours later, sitting on the sidelines as the Leone regaled us with stories of what they'd done in the years that had passed since Felice's last visit. We reciprocated with tales of our own observations and adventures, which were received with effusive thanks.

Fáolán was surrounded by cubs both in human and Leone form, and was clearly having the time of his life. The youngsters seemed to be as enchanted with him as he was with them. When their chattering became loud enough to drown out the sounds of adult conversation, he shepherded them over to a circle of logs fifty feet or so away from the main gathering and sat down to tell them stories of his life.

It was difficult not to go over and listen to his tales, but somehow, I stayed with the grownups.

"We aren't staying long," I told Hans' mate, a sweet female called Gertrude. "We have to find some friends of ours, and we need to find them as quickly as possible. Time is of the essence, if we're to keep them from being ended."

"Felice keeps more than one of her planes here," Gertrude told me. "I'm certain she will be using one of those to reach your destination as quickly as is practicable. There is one or two of the clan whom she has taught to fly the things, so it will be brought back here, should such a thing become necessary."

Trust one of the Leone females to have sense. The males were such preening creatures that one could almost accuse them of being flighty.

But only if you really want to get bitten.

Eleven

So, the next morning, after a good long sleep in one of the Leone's few walled residences, and then a hot bath, we set off in Beechcraft Bonanza six seater plane that was the antithesis of the Learjet in which we'd escaped from Jordan. Sometime during the night, the Learjet had been moved into a battered old airplane hangar to remain concealed until next Felice required its services, while this one had been wheeled into its place.

Felice had hugged several of the Leone before we departed. I could see that she cared about them far more than she cared to let on. I could understand that feeling, myself. Being part of a Leone clan, even if you were non-Leone, was something not easily brushed aside, emotionally.

Several of the cubs crowded around Fáolán to bid him goodbye, and I could see the sadness in his eyes as he was forced to part from them all. In our short acquaintance, he had never struck me as a sentimental sort, but it appeared that he was quite taken with the revelation that the Leone were still alive and well. Thinking about it, I realized that he had likely seen the birth and death of more than one civilization, so it was probably something of a relief to see one erased from the list of "lost" peoples.

Oh, we'd gained another member of our merry little party. One of the Leone, a female called Ilse, had been chosen to accompany us. She was quite small for one of her kind, but her clansmen were effusive in their praise for her hunting and killing abilities. She had been through a lot of the European continent in her twenty-three years of life, so she knew the lay of the land, so to speak. It would be a great help to us to have her along. While in the plane, which was designed to seat six, she had shifted to her Leone form and was curled up in the rear, eschewing being strapped into one of the seats. If you did not know she was Leone, you'd think we had a black panther loose in the plane.

We had not planned on having a Leone come along with us, but she had argued her case most persuasively and we had finally relented. She refused to take "No" for an answer. Other considerations had also come up, and we could not ignore them.

"I can slip in and out of places without being noticed," she had argued.

"She's smaller than any of the other Leone here," her mother, a stocky female called Marva commented. "She has not yet found a mate here in the clan. Perhaps she will be able to find one out in the world. I only worry that she may be discovered out in the world of the humans."

"I will keep an eye on her, lady Marva," came from a surprising set of vocal cords. "I will keep her as safe as I possibly may."

Fáolán stepped forward and put a hand on Ilse's mother's own, squeezing it gently.

"I will watch over as though she were my own daughter," he promised her.

"You don't have any offspring, vampire," Marva stated flatly. "I do know that much about you."

"I will keep her safe," Fáolán insisted, putting a hand on that worthy's slender shoulder and staring into her golden eyes.

"I know that you will do the best you can to keep her safe, as you put it," Marva replied, "But you can only do so much. We Leone either live or die, with the strongest surviving to create the next generation. Such will be the same with our Ilse."

Marva suddenly shifted to her Leone form, licked Ilse's cheek once, roughly, then turned her back on all of us and walked back to where the rest of the clan waited quietly. Whatever had happened, Ilse had been dismissed from the clan and was now officially our problem. Ilse, looking a little hurt at what was obviously a dismissal from her mother, straightened up and put a resolute expression on her face as she looked at us, her new clan members.

"I will be sure to pull my weight, clan mother," she said to me formally, taking my hand in her own and licking it once, hard. "My meat is your meat."

Clan mother? When the hell had *that* happened? I had one offspring already, and certainly was not looking for another, vampire, Leone or anything else, for that matter.

"When was the last time you saw one of the Leone, Fáolán," Nathaniel asked him as we forged out way through the air. "You said before that you had thought them extinct."

"In the eleventh century," Fáolán replied, looking back over his shoulder to where Ilse napped. "I had met them while I was free after my third escape. They gave me shelter for several decades before the Council found me once more, shuttling me between one clan and another as the years passed. The one who I had thought to be the last of this race was called Enulf. He was a friend."

"Does your being a clan mother make her my sister now," Nathaniel asked me. If I had seen anything like mischief in his eyes, I'd have slapped him, but I saw only serious thoughts reflected there, for a change. "How does that work?"

"Yes, in a way, she is your sister," I responded. "You saw how the Leone society works while we were in the Middle East. Overall, they all consider each other to be family. In this case, as Ilse has left her family and joined us, I have taken over as her clan mother. Her natural mother, has given her over into our care, and as far as she's concerned, Ilse is now dead."

"Dead? Why dead?" Nathaniel blurted out.

"Ilse can no longer help to keep safe and maintain her old clan, since she decided to go with us, so she has removed herself from her old clan," I told him. "She's become part of ours, even though we obviously aren't Leone. Her psyche demands that she be part of a larger group, so we are that for her, and you are essentially her brother."

"How can that be," Nathaniel protested. "She's not a vampire."

"That has nothing to do with it, Nathaniel," I said. "This is how things are within their society. You are to treat her as family from now on. She will be doing the same where you are concerned, so keep that in mind."

I saw the confusion on his face, but also knew him well enough to understand that he would obey me in this. I wondered if vampires went through this odd jealousy with their older offspring when they made new vampires. Glancing over, I saw that Ilse's eyes were closed, but her twitching ears let me know that she was listening to our conversation. I wondered what was going on in her own head now. This had to be at least as unnerving for her as it was for us vampires. I believe that she was more comfortable in her feline form than her human form, judging from the amount of time she spent on four legs, rather than two.

Fáolán clearly was not happy with my apparent elevation to clan mother in the eyes of the young Leone, but as their society was a matriarchy, it made perfect sense that Ilse had sworn her allegiance to me. He had not actually said anything out loud, but I could see the confusion and hurt on his own face when he thought no one was looking.

Conversation died in the plane for a while, each of us lost in our own thoughts. Felice was in the pilot's seat, but Nathaniel, in the co-pilot's seat, was actually flying the plane. The former was dozing lightly while she had the chance. It wouldn't be all that long before we would land in Belgium to take care of some pressing business.

"What can we expect when we land," I asked. "I haven't taken a private plane into a European airport in decades."

"I don't plan to land at a commercial airport in Belgium," Felice said, opening her eyes and turning her head in order to look at me. "There is a small airport a few miles from where we need to go where

I have landing privileges. They've been notified that I'll be there soon and will have a vehicle ready for our use."

"How do you manage all this preparation and still remain incognito," Fáolán wanted to know. "I would think that everyone would know you."

"They know me under a variety of names, but not as Felice," she told him. "I created a network a very long time ago, and all of them know enough not to ask too many questions. They're also very well paid for their reticence."

"It sounds like a private Haven," Nathaniel noted. "Siofra has told me about them, but I haven't actually seen one yet."

"I suppose it does," Felice allowed. "Whatever it is, it's been a great boon to me."

"When did you start putting it together?" I asked her. "You've never said anything about them to me, and I've known you for what seems like forever."

"Oh, probably about thirty years after my supposed ending. I kept their existence from you because I wanted to avoid any chance of anyone else finding out about them. I created them because I got tired of having to make do for myself, and started creating permanent safe places. I've only had to abandon a few of them since that time. Usually because political issues made my remaining in an area too dangerous."

"Political issues?" Nathaniel asked.

"Oh, I used to have places all over the Middle East, but those are much fewer now," she replied. "As the extremists have extended their hold over so much of the area, it's much more difficult for a single female to pass through unremarked, and I don't have the time or the energy to fight my way out of those types of situations. I have a place in Amman, Jordan, so that made our meeting a bit easier."

"Sounds like it," Nathaniel said. "I'm not really sure what Siofra has set up around the world."

"I have a few places," I said. "They're supported by a Trust, so I don't have to have direct control of finances to keep them around. One of them is in France, or was, the last time I looked. I'm assuming the Council has them under surveillance, so it's not safe for me to visit any of them."

"I was going to wait to say anything, Siofra, but your place in Nancy has been obliterated. I think it was one of the first places the Council sent their goons when they decided to end you," Felice said quietly. "I heard about it through the grapevine."

"Why did not you say anything before?" I demanded. "I could have helped them, maybe!"

"A few of your humans did escape, but only because they were away on some religious holiday or something. Your manager was not quite so lucky."

"What's that supposed to mean?"

"Like the Captain of a ship, he stayed to make sure that everyone got out," Felice said softly. "Then he blew it up, taking most of the squad of assassins with him."

"How'd you find that out?" Nathaniel asked her.

"I hired on a few of them after it happened. Your manager's wife and two daughters are now living at one of my private refuges," she replied. "Surprisingly, she doesn't hate you, so you must have done something to make them like you."

"I'm not sure what that could have been," I told her. "I did not see them very much at all. They just had to make sure it would be available if and when I needed it."

"Maybe that was it, Siofra," Nathaniel said to me. "You gave them a stable life and home. That's always worth something."

Conversation died and I spent a long time thinking of Pierre LePetit, who had been the manager of my place in Nancy for at least the past forty years. I had known him as a dedicated and honorable human, and it hurt to know that he was gone, but I was also proud of him for what he had done in allowing so many to escape. His family had been serving mine since the time of his great grandmother, and he was not the first of that line to have given his life in my service. Pierre had always known that I would take care of his wife and children as long as they lived in the event that he made that ultimate sacrifice.

Twelve

We landed at another private airport not too far from our destination, and piled into a beat up little Fiat 500 to finish things. The car smelled of age and sweat, its upholstery torn, and the uncomfortable seat springs straining to escape their leathery prison. I felt the most sympathy for our little Leone friend, who could not heal as we did. Her final decision was to lie across Nathaniel's and Fáolán's laps in the rear seat, still in her Leone form. It was fortunate indeed that in her Leone form, she was easily only about half the mass of her clan mates, so her weight was not too rough on her unconventional perches.

I wondered if some of the Leone were making an evolutionary change, which would explain why this one was as small as she was. The clans we'd known in the Middle East tended to be both large in their humanoid forms as well as their Leone forms. As humanoids, they tended to be well fleshed out humans of notable size, which reflected their size when they shifted into their Leone aspects. The only other assumption was that this one was a sport, and that if she did not get the chance to mate, this smaller breed of Leone might be lost entirely.

We meandered up a narrow dirt road before Felice pulled over, parking the vehicle amongst a group of dead and dying trees and shrubs. The evening shadows plunged the area into near darkness once the car's lights were switched off.

"We're going to have to walk from here," she said. "Last I knew, he had guards patrolling the grounds, and each of them have a radio to keep in touch with their fellows. Somehow, we're going to have to get through them in order to get to him."

"Are you sure he's still here?" Nathaniel asked her. "He could always have gone elsewhere."

"Alan Beaudalaire doesn't move around very much, Nathaniel," she told him. "He likes staying close to familiar territory, and he runs all of this like his own little fiefdom. He nearly runs the local human Council as well. They'd be well rid of him if we're able to take him out."

"Do you know how many guards he's got?" I asked. "There seem to be a few too many unknowns here. I don't want to find myself ducking bullets or worse when we get in there."

"That I could not tell you, Siofra," she replied. "Numbers change all the time. This one tends to keep humans, rather than other vampires. I don't even believe he's got any offspring."

"Yes, he has one, Felice," Fáolán said from the back seat. "She was calling herself Serena, the last time I heard anything about her. She has had very little to do with him in the time since she joined Klaus' kiss a few hundred years ago."

"Very little? What happened to cause that," she asked, surprised. "They always seemed to be very close."

"He tried to have Klaus ended, and she took it personally, seeing as she'd been in lust with Klaus for several decades. It took an action of the entire Council to keep them from going to war," he told her. "Indeed, it came very close to that happening. I believe the Council might have simply allowed them to take their feud to its logical end, but there were other considerations at the time."

"What in the world could have made them force a peace between them." Felice asked

him. "The Council cares about little except themselves and their place in the Council's hierarchy."

"Money, of course. Each of the warring kisses have a large amount of money between them, and the Council felt that they had a better chance of getting their hands on more of it with the principals still existing rather than wrangling what they could of it after they'd ended one another," he explained. "In the end, he tried to force Serena to return to him, but the Council decided that she did not have to do that.

They felt that with her in Klaus' kiss, it would remind her maker to mind his manners."

"You've gleaned all of this information during the time you've been the Council's record keeper," I said to him. "I can't imagine how you can hold onto all of that information."

"Oh, it's not just what I told you now," he said. "It's every word that was ever spoken on the subject in my hearing. The tone of each voice, the facial expressions, even what people were wearing when things happened. I'll even remember our conversation that we're having right now. I can't help but remember it. There is no on and off switch for me."

I could not help shuddering as he reminded me of his curse. Yes, it would be nice to have a good memory, but a good memory is much different than what Fáolán had experienced for somewhere around a millennium.

It did not take long before we encountered the first patrol, which consisted of two burly, parka-clad human males armed with machine pistols. They were not being careless. I could see that at a glance. One of them kept his hand on his radio mic's button, ready to report anything out of the ordinary. Their heartbeats were slow and regular, meaning that neither was nervous. We'd have to take out the one with his hand on his radio, first.

Ilse slipped into the darkness, her black coat helping to conceal her far more than her mother's tawny coat would have in the same situation. The dappled pattern that was barely visible in the moonlight was a great aid in allowing her to move through the shadows. It seemed as though she disappeared and became just another part of the shadows. A human would be unable to hear her cotton-soft footfalls as she picked her way through the dried leaves and twigs that littered the ground.

With the flick of an ear in Nathaniel's direction, she leapt forward silently, neatly taking half the flesh of the human's throat away in her mouth as she did so, his blood gushing out in a thick red river. He never even had the chance to scream, only making a gurgling sound as he fought his death.

At the same time, Nathaniel made his own leap and twisted the other guard's head around backward, breaking the man's neck, and then dropped the corpse down to the ground. I felt regret that we had to waste so much blood, but we did not have time to drink them down. We needed to get in and out of Alan's place and on our way as quickly as possible.

I heard the sound of tearing fabric and turned to see Ilse, still busy with her victim, ripping open the dead human's heavy jacket to get at the soft belly skin underneath. She then raked at the corpse's cooling skin with her ridiculously sharp claws, revealing the filth-filled entrails to the cool night air.

Ilse sat back a moment, waiting for me to say something. It was her kill, and it was her right to consume the tasty treats, but she first looked at me, her acknowledged clanmother, for permission to do so.

"Its fine, Ilse. It's not as though I could eat it, anyway," I told her, gesturing at her with one hand. "Enjoy! Once they're dead, I have no use for them. The meat will always be yours to do with as you wish."

With these words of release, Ilse buried her face in the hole she had made and ripped out a steaming length of intestines before expertly reaching in further with a claw and tearing out kidneys, liver and other organs. Perhaps it would have been best to not allow her to feed, but I was not too worried about it. The Leone used a massive amount of energy when they shifted, and it was important that she regain as much of that energy as she could as quickly as possible.

Ilse gulped the steaming organs down in great chunks, only stopping once they were gone and then leaving the rest of the body to cool in the night air. Her enormous pink tongue emerged from her mouth to clean her face an incongruous splash of color against the midnight darkness of her coat. I could tell, just from watching her, that if she had had the opportunity to play with the human before killing him, she would have taken it. While the Leone might have a humanoid aspect, that did not make them any less the big cats they were.

"Ilse, you move out and see what you can see. If they're on their own, only take them out if you know you can do it safely. We don't want any accidents this early in the game," I told her. She flattened her ears for a moment in acknowledgement and then slipped back into the darkness on her errand of merry mayhem. "No more stopping to eat. We need to get through all of this and deal with Alan before he knows what's going on."

Nathaniel carried his victim deep into the bushes to conceal it, and Fáolán did the same with the one who Ilse had eviscerated, careful to keep as much of the gore off his skin and clothing. The scent of death filled the air around us, and we could not kill every human that we encountered, as convenient as that might make things for us. We might be able to get away with killing a few on the fringes of the property, but too much death would catch our prey's attention, and that's the last thing that we wanted.

Felice had slipped along behind Ilse to help with subduing the human guards. She understood the importance of keeping bloodshed to a minimum...for now. We'd feast when it was all over with, and knowing what we faced, a lot of that blood would go to healing us of whatever wounds we accumulated during our face to face with Alan.

It had been a very long time since last I had faced him, and the last time had not ended very well at all. For either of us. Of course, at that time, white phosphorus grenades had not been invented yet, either.

We only had to end one other patrolling guard as we approached the main house. That had been one who'd absolutely refused to surrender. Perhaps he knew that we would be ending all of them, anyway, once we were finished with Alan. None of us could afford to leave any of them alive to go running, squealing, to the Council.

We had not accomplished the neutralization of the guards without damage. Fáolán's face had been torn by one of the humans when he slipped a knife from his boot and attempted to stick the wicked thing in the vampire's left eye socket. His face was sliced open from his lower eyelid, down to and through his upper lip, leaving behind a particularly gruesome wound. The white bone of his skull was exposed, as well as the severed musculature beneath his skin.

A stream of archaic invective had vomited from Fáolán's ruined mouth as he bent the human's knife hand far enough backward that we all heard the sharp report as his radius and ulna snapped. The knife dropped to the ground with a dull thump, Fáolán's fluids shining along its sharp edge.

We were lucky that the human passed out from the pain, or he might have made more than the high-pitched squeal he had uttered before descending into insensibility. The ugly look on Fáolán's face made it very apparent what was going to happen next.

"This little *mac soith* cut me!" he snarled, leaning in toward the human's neck. His left eye looked odd, as the muscles beneath it had been severed, and the left corner of his mouth sagged a bit. "I'm not going anywhere with half my face hanging off. He's going to fix this!"

"You can't kill him yet!" Felice stepped in, putting a hand on his chest. "Take as much as you need to heal, but don't end him. We've got enough of the stink of death out here already. Too much more, and that shit just might notice it. Honestly, I'm surprised he's not investigating things already!"

Fáolán looked at the diminutive vampire, appearing as though he might strike out at her, but then he seemed to hear what she was saying and moved from the human's throat to the inner fold of his elbow. Nicking the fat vein with a fang, he applied his mouth to the wound and drank gently for a few moments.

We all watched as Fáolán's damaged face knitted itself back together, first the muscles flowing together again, and then his skin moving to mend itself. When the process was ended, he was left unscarred and exotically beautiful once again. He pulled a pristine handkerchief from the sleeve of his tunic and used it as a tourniquet to stop the human's blood loss. Fáolán was such a fop that the shiny clean handkerchief really did not surprise me much, but the human did not need anything that clean to keep him alive.

It was not as though he was going to survive much beyond the ending of his master, but it was best to have as much blood as possible on hand in the event we experienced any more damage than we had already.

The surviving guards, now gagged, were carried away to a far point of the property, where they were handcuffed to trees. Knowing that humans could be very creative in a pinch, we made sure they were restrained far enough from each other that they would not be able to combine their efforts in an attempt to free themselves.

Working our way through several key rings we had taken from the guards, we finally found the key that opened the back kitchen entrance to the mansion. The lone human cook we found took one look at us, muttered a plea for mercy and scuttled on out the back door and into the night, in the opposite direction from the one we had come.

Ilsa purred a question at me, and I shook my head. There was no reason to end the cook, as that worthy was obviously uninterested in defending its territory, and judging by his direction, he was not going to run into the guards we'd secured outside. Thus, we moved on, stepping as silently on the marble floors as we could.

The one human was the only living creature we found in the building. I assumed that Alan kept a cook to feed his security men, as he had the same dietary restrictions we observed. It did surprise me, however, that I found no other servants caring for the property. At the very least, some kind of majordomo to oversee things and free Alan from those obligations.

We explored a large portion of the place before Ilsa sneezed and nodded in one direction, making a big business of sniffing the air.

Inhaling for the first time in at least an hour, I found I could smell the vaguest scent of decay. What in the world was going on here?

"This way," I whispered gesturing to the others and falling in behind Ilsa's velvety blackness. "Something's not right."

We only made it a few steps before that vague scent became a sudden tidal wave of revolting stench. At the head of that wave was Alan, covered in dried, rotting blood eyes wild. The sound of Ilsa's sneeze must have gotten his attention. At least we did not have to hunt for him anymore.

"What do you think, you are doing here?" He demanded, taking in all of us with a wave of his filthy hand. "Leave at once! Guards!"

"Your guards aren't able to help you, asshole," I told him, staring him directly in the eye, refusing to back down. "You and I have something to discuss."

"You! You're supposed to be ended!" He yelled as he beheld me and I saw recognition cross his face. "The Council swore that you were ended!"

"Hardly," I replied. "I'm tougher than you thought."

Alan was gibbering now, terror in his eyes. Why was he so frightened? It did not make any sense to me.

He leapt at me with murder in his eye and Nathaniel intercepted him, snarling, knocking the older vampire backward. My companions ranged out behind me, but made no other move toward Alan.

"I'm not that easy to end, Alan," I sneered. "I've got some questions for you, and you're going to be forthcoming, too."

"Fuck off!" he screamed at me, and turned to run the other direction.

We took off after him as he ran through back the way he had come, the stench of death becoming even stronger than it had been before, if such a thing were possible. Glad that I did not have to breathe, I stopped, but felt a little guilty that Ilsa had no such good fortune to protect her very sensitive nose.

Following Alan into a final entryway and racing downstairs, we abruptly discovered where the horrendous odor was coming from, and it was not pretty.

Piles of human bodies in various stages of decay lined the walls, maggots wriggling in ecstasy as they devoured the rotting flesh. Ilsa's nose was wrinkled in disgust as we beheld the carnage before us. From the clothing that remained on the bodies, I could see where they servants had got to, and none of the house servants, it appeared (beyond the cook, that is), appeared to have come to a good end.

It also made me wonder why the cook had even remained on the property. Had he been so obtuse that he had not figured out what was going on with his fellow employees as they disappeared, one by one? Or had he simply not cared about his own safety?

"This is just disgusting," Felice said, voicing what I believe was the opinion of us all. "How can he live like this?"

"I have no idea. He was a much more fastidious vampire when I knew him," Fáolán volunteered. "What could have driven him to this extreme?"

"Maybe we'll be able to find out," I suggested. "We have to find him first, though."

It took a little bit, but we found him cringing behind a pile of corpses, trying to make himself look as inconspicuous as possible. Ilse prowled the room, sniffing deeply and trying to differentiate the stench of decomposition from that of the vampire.

His trembling was what finally gave him away, since only the maggots were trembling on the dead bodies that surrounded him. The Leone raked him with her claws, making him cry out in pain and make a futile attempt to escape. Fáolán stepped forward and clamped a hand on Alan's filthy collar, pulling him away from the filthy corpses and into our little group.

"Fáolán!" Alan blurted out as he realized who held him. "I thought you were still caged."

"I was, until my latest keeper got a little too close for his own safety. It's always a bad idea to walk around with your keys dangling from your belt." Fáolán replied. "I've been out in the world again for the past little while. I don't intend to go back into that cage again."

Alan appeared to ignore Fáolán's words, as he had begun to mutter to himself.

"I told them they needed to make sure she was too wily to be ended so easily! But no, they wouldn't listen to me and now look what's happened!" he said to himself in a crazed tone of voice. "These modern vampires are too wily by far!"

"Alan, what do you mean?" I asked him, catching his chin and forcing him to look at me. "Who are 'they'?"

His wide eyes slid away and looked sideways toward the rotting flesh next to him, his blubbering never coming to a halt. Actually watching a vampire slide into madness made me feel a bit sick inside, and I felt a rising horror at the sight. I had never seen it happen before, although I had heard about it from other vampires who'd seen it happen.

"Oh, Janos, I should never have listened to them! I should have stood away from it all and left them to their own endings," he babbled to the half-rotted face that grinned senselessly at him, its one remaining eyeball covered with a milky film.

Alan put a hand on the corpse's cheek and jostle it as if cajoling it to listen and understand his point. His gesture caused dozens of maggots to tumble from the cold damp flesh on which they fed, sending them to the filthy floor to wriggle in distress. It made me angry to hear him even utter Janos' name, as though he was not good enough to use it.

"I thought if I stayed inside, I'd be safe!" Alan cried out.

Safe? He had somehow gone down the dark road into insanity, and this stinking nightmare was the result. I felt no pity for him, knowing that my original intent stood and that I would be ending him once I had the information I required.

"Alan," Nathaniel cut in front of me and grabbed the vampire by the blood-crusted lace of his blouse. "Who else is involved in this?"

Appearing to be confused at the sound of this new voice, Alan turned his head, his eyes focusing on Nathaniel's face, his brow wrinkling as he tried to gather his thoughts. At least, that's how it looked to me. For just a breath of a moment, coherence flooded his face and he managed a sensible reply.

"Margarethe, of course, and her fawning pet, Ri'chard," he replied. "Who are you? I don't know you."

"In a moment. Who else is involved?" Nathaniel demanded, doubling the fistful of cloth in his hand and jerking Alan off the ground to pull him within an inch's distance from his face. "Tell me now!"

Alan's eyes widened in fear and then the babbling resumed, this time with absolutely no rhyme or reason to it. I shook my head. We'd lost him completely, and while I was pissed, I did feel a very small amount of pity that he would not be sane enough to appreciate the ending he faced.

"Nathaniel, I don't think you're going to get anything else out of him. I know the vampires to whom he referred, and I have at least an idea of who would follow their lead on this pogrom," I told him, reaching up and using my hand to gently push him own down so that Alan's feet once again touched the floor. "I just realized whose voice it was on the phone after Janos was murdered."

"You do?" Felice asked.

"Mikhail."

Thirteen

I could not help glancing out the car's rear window once again to see Alan's mansion being consumed in the violently hot flames created by the phosphorus grenade. It glowed brightly behind a thick curtain of smoke, but it still gave me a certain level of satisfaction to see what I could of the destruction, even though I knew that the chemicals created by the stuff would wreck holy hell on any human or wildlife in its path.

At one point, I fancied hearing Alan's agonized screams as he was ended, but knew there was little chance of my hearing that. We'd torn off his legs at the knee joint to keep him from crawling away and perhaps escaping. I'm sure the manacle we put on his wrist helped with that as well.

Alan did not even seem to realize what was going on when we chained him to the front pillar of his mansion and tossed a couple phosphorus grenades in his general direction. . The white phosphorous burned so hot that not even whatever rudimentary fire suppression system the place had would be unable to put it out. The stuff is just entirely too nasty for that. Animals and humans in the vicinity stood a great chance of being injured or killed by the chemical fallout of the incendiary device, but I did not care. The mansion rested on an enormous plot of land in a lightly inhabited part of the country.

Are you shocked at my indifference to any potential loss of human life? Need I again remind you that I'm a sinner not a saint? If the humans who lived downwind of the smoke had at least a modicum of intelligence, they'd get the hell out of it as quickly as they could.

One of my enemies was ended, and it was time to move on to the next target on my list. The intense heat of the white phosphorous-ignited conflagration would destroy all evidence of the massive pile of rotting corpses that Alan had created, which would keep forensic surprises to a minimum. We'd fed well from the captive guards before tossing their corpses into the merry blaze, there was no sense in wasting the opportunity.

"Have you heard anything about where Margarethe nests?" I asked Fáolán. "That bitch's time is over!"

"I have heard of several residences over the centuries. I do not know how many she frequents at this time, or if they all continue to exist. Unless we are able to find confirmation of her location, we will have to go door to door, as it were, until we are able to locate her current hideaway," he told me with a shrug.

"And here I thought you were this super vampire," I sputtered, irritated at his dismissive attitude. "Go through that computer of a brain of yours and see if you can find any specifics, anything that will help to locate her."

"I'm not a damned computer, Siofra," he snapped at me. "I'm not just a tool for you to use! I've been used as a tool for centuries now, and I have fucking had it! You'd best remember that."

"Fáolán, I'm sorry that I hurt your feelings," I responded. "but we need to figure this out before she has a chance to bug out on us. I'm sorry that you've been through this pile of bullshit with the Council, but I would think that taking them out would be foremost on your list of things to do. Am I wrong?"

Fáolán stared at me, his mouth twisted in a rictus of anger. I think if he had been able to do so, his face would have been red with his anger. Instead, that anger was reflected in his eyes and the flash of his fangs as he snarled at me. In its tight atmosphere of the little car's passenger cabin, he was rendered even more intimidating. Even I felt a little fear, deep inside myself, and was gladdened that Nathaniel could no longer pick up on my emotions.

"I know you're sorry Siofra, but you need to be aware that I'm more than just a recording device. I'm a person. I have feelings. And as I said, I'm not a tool. I'm not a computer. I'm another vampire, not quite just like you, but like you, I have feelings. Never forget that. Ever."

"Fáolán, I'm really not trying to piss you off. Truly. I just know that Margarethe is very good at getting information," I told him. "I don't need her spies telling her that Alan has been ended. That will just cause Margarethe to put her guard up and make it that much more difficult to end her."

"You think she won't know something's up when she hears that Alan is not only ended, but his entire mansion has been burned to the ground? Are you really that dense?" Fáolán demanded of me. "You're a foolish child if you think she's not going to know that something stinks."

"If we move fast enough, Fáolán, she might not have the chance to hear about it before we end her," I protested.

"That's wishful thinking, and you know it," he said quietly. "I know you're angry about what happened to Janos and what these vampires tried to do to you, but you have to think things through better than you apparently have. This isn't just going to affect you. This is going to affect everyone who agrees to help you."

He was right and I was wrong, but I was still pissed off at him and clamped my mouth shut, unwilling to reply. We rode on in an uncomfortable silence, Nathaniel behind the wheel with Felice next to him. Ilse lay across my and Fáolán's laps, staying very quiet and still, obviously trying to keep from becoming included in our disagreement.

When we got to where the plane was hidden, Fáolán and I were the last ones out of the car, Ilse having leapt out as soon as the car door was open. Nathaniel and Felice had not said a word before getting out and going to the plane to get things underway. Were Fáolán and I really being so completely ridiculous and stubborn that no one wanted to speak to us? It certainly seemed to be that way, and I did not much like it.

"I'm sorry if I'm not being fair to you, Fáolán," I told him. "I know I'm heavily focused on all of this and ending these bastards, and I have to be more thoughtful with the people around me."

He stared at the seat back in front of him for a minute or two before turning to look at me.

"You and I are both stubborn," he replied in a surprisingly conciliatory manner. "We're older than a lot of other vampires, and we're used to doing things our own way. It's a little different for me, as I've been a living chronicler for the Council against my will for longer than several of those Council members have been vampires. When I'm out on my own, I tend to be less understanding when people ask things of me. I'll try to be better than that."

He put out a hand and held it there, clearly wanting to ease things between us. I took the proffered hand and shook it firmly. We had a lot to do in a very short period of time, and being at odds with one another was not going to help the situation at all.

I climbed out of the car and made my way to the plane and then climbed inside. Felice had already started the engine and we had no time to dawdle. Fáolán came in right behind me and pulled the door shut, latching it tightly behind him.

"Look, guys, I'm sorry that we got into it in the car. I'm going to try to be better about that, but it was not fair that you were caught up in my stupidity," I said to Felice and Nathaniel. "I hope you can forgive me."

No one said anything from the cockpit beyond normal flight-related talk, so I took a seat in the passenger cabin next to where Fáolán had chosen to sit. Hopefully we'd be able to work out what was going to happen next.

"We need to get out of these clothes," Fáolán said. "The stench of the dead tends to be oily and has permeated what we have on."

"I'd prefer you all sat still back there," Felice said from her place in the pilot's seat. "This bag of struts and bolts isn't anywhere near as sturdy as the Lear. You can change once we land again."

"Where will we be landing next time?" I asked her. "We really haven't talked about that much."

"You said you have contacts in England, so we'll land there. When I was there about twenty years ago or so, there was a private airfield near Sheffield. If we're lucky, it'll still be there when we arrive," she told us. "We'll figure out transportation from there."

Nathaniel still had not said a word to me, and I wondered if I had somehow damaged our relationship during my spat with Fáolán. As soon as I had the chance, I would take him aside to have that conversation. I did not want to do it here, in public as it were. Nathaniel's and my relationship was nobody's business but our own.

Rather than discuss anything, I leaned back and closed my eyes to rest while I could. I was tired after our recent adventuring, despite feeding before we set fire to everything. While blood was both healing and nourishing, it was still no substitute for sleep, so I had have to catch up sometime. Our flight wouldn't take us more than a couple hours to complete, so sleeping was a good plan, especially as Fáolán's and my reconciliation was still fresh. I did not want to once again stick my foot in my mouth with him.

Fourteen

The flight had been uneventful and the van we'd rented once we landed was serviceable. Although it could easily handle three benches full of passengers, we'd had the helpful employee at the agency remove the rear one to enable us to haul more supplies with us.

Ilse had regained her human form, if only to avoid terrorizing the human who assisted us in obtaining the vehicle, but once we returned to the road, she went feline again and returned to dozing atop the bags that lay in the space vacated by the unneeded bench seat. Warm sunlight poured in the back window as we drove, so I could understand her very catlike desire to bask in it while she could. Protracted sunlight could be rare in Great Britain, and in fact, the country was famous more for its rain than its sunny days. It had even been sung about on at least one occasion.

I had an idea of where I might be able to find some help, too. I'd inadvertently set that up years before while trying to be helpful to someone else. Funny how sometimes, things seem to come full circle that way.

After getting in touch with his guardians through an intermediary, I was able to get Ali's cell number, and I gave him a call. His enthusiastic greeting was something I'd cherish.

"Miss Siofra!" he enthused in a voice at least twice as deep has it had been when last we had spoken. "Of course I would be more than willing to be of any assistance I could possibly offer!"

I should have hated myself for what I said next, but I didn't. I knew that I wouldn't get an argument from him, since I knew he felt obligated to me.

"We need a safe place to stay while we work to find out what's going on here," I told him. "Where can we meet you?"

"I will be at my home in Kensington in an hour's time, if that will suit your needs," he responded. "You have done so very much for me, Miss Siofra. I am happy to render you what little aid I am able."

"Has university gone well for you, then," I asked, although I knew the answer already, as I'd been closely watching his university career. One does that when one is the vampire footing the bills. I wouldn't have tolerated a party-boy, and had been gratified to discover that he was a determined student not given to fraternization with his peers. "I know you left your people with lofty goals in mind."

"Indeed it has, and my people are never far from my mind," he told me. "I have been doing a study on genetics to find out how best to help us survive. There aren't enough resources in the areas in which most of us currently live. There simply isn't enough meat to go around."

I knew that his "us" referred to the Leone, and had nothing to do with vampires. He was a Leone who did not shift, so he had been essentially ostracized from his community. They weren't mean about it, but had encouraged him to find another place in the world. It wasn't the most forward-thinking thing his people could have done, but Ali wasn't the kind of person to hold a grudge. Instead of taking their shunning personally, he was working to help his people survive. I hoped that at some point, they would realize this and recognize his work.

The Leone's diet consisted primarily of meat protein. While they could consume vegetation, it wasn't something their bodies could utilize very successfully. It acted more as a filler, but wouldn't sate the hunger in the same manner that meat would do. Unless they could satisfactorily adapt to a modified diet or could survive on less meat, they would slowly starve to death. Then I had an idea that was so perfect, it was as though Fate had arranged for it to occur.

"I have someone you should meet, Ali. It may give you something to consider with your study," I told him, thinking of Ilsa. "I think it's important."

"Meet someone? What do you—?"

"You'll find out when we see you shortly. Until then, Ali," I told him. "See you soon!"

"Who is this Ali to whom you refer," Fáolán asked me as I disconnected. "You haven't mentioned him before. Can he be trusted?"

"Ali is one of the Leone, but one who does not shift. I arranged for him to travel to England when it became apparent this was the case," I told him. "I assure you that he is completely trustworthy."

"He doesn't shift? The Leone I knew would have killed him for lacking this ability," he told us all. "They only allowed those who could shift to survive to breed another generation of Leone."

"Well, they've obviously decided that this wasn't the best way to do things," Nathaniel shot back from where he sat. "Killing him off would be like exposing a disabled infant or child."

"Only the strongest survive that way," Fáolán replied. "It has been thus with some cultures for millennia, even until today."

"It's a foolish practice, especially when your people are in danger of disappearing entirely. The Leone I know apparently decided that this wasn't the way to be," I told him. "If he was to reproduce with one of his people there is every chance that at least one of his offspring would be a shifter."

The ancient vampire grumped a bit from the back seat but didn't say anything else as we drove. Fáolán's instinctual distrust was understandable, but had grown old enough to irritate me.

"He does not shift," Ilsa piped her question from her place in the rear of the vehicle. I looked in the rear view mirror to see a bizarre creature with both human and feline features. Ilsa had shifted back to human form just enough to participate in the conversation. I'd never seen another Leone accomplish something like that, but that didn't mean she was unusual, only that the Leone hadn't shared that ability with me. "How sad. I do not think I could accept it if I was unable to do so."

"It doesn't make him any less of a Leone," I chided her in a voice that wasn't very kind at all. She could be a pompous little shit, and I saw no reason for her to maintain her inflated sense of value. "Except for some minor differences having to do with being able to shift, you have the same DNA. Perhaps between the two of you, you might be able to save your species."

"I think I would have killed myself," she muttered from the back seat, just loud enough for me to hear her, and I looked back at her through the rear view mirror and gave her a dirty look.

"Well, I'm glad that Ali didn't feel that way," I shot back, and she averted her eyes from mine, deciding not to challenge me. "He's got a lot to offer your people, of whom you are both members, with what he's learning at university."

I continued to watch her in the rear view as she shifted back to full feline form, clearly disinterested in continuing the conversation. The young Leone had better pull her paw out of her ass, if she wanted her people to continue more than a few additional generations.

From that point, silence ruled in the vehicle except for the occasional comment from the turn-by-turn GPS mapping program as it directed us to our destination. We were nearly to Kensington and a safe haven, at least for now.

The GPS' directions missed a street and we had to do a bit of backtracking before we finally located it. The cloudy sky was dark and only a few streetlights showed their light on the street, and that fitfully. Except for those relative few whose livelihoods required they be awake at this time of night, all other sane humans were already abed and deep in slumber.

Leaving the vehicle parked tightly along the side of the road, we all made our way to the front door of a small stone cottage, Ilsa stubbornly accompanying us in her Leone form. Fortunately, the night was dark, so she easily became a part of the shadows, eyes alert, nostrils flaring and her ears twitching at every tiny sound.

Before I could even knock, the door flew open, and I saw Ali framed in it, his eyes wide with welcome and something else that looked like...fear? Ilsa snarled, started forward, and then came to an abrupt halt as Ali stepped into her, which only confused me even more. As I gathered myself to attack whatever this new threat was, someone stepped out from the hallway and into my field of vision.

Estelle. And boy did she look pissed.

Glossary:

Dearg (*noun Gaelic* Djareg) red

Droch Fola (*Gaelic*) bad blood

Fáolán (*Gaelic* FAY'lun) - little wolf

Mac soith (*Irish Gaelic epithet* mahk soy') - "Son of a bitch"

Mathúin (*noun Gaelic* MAH hoon) Bear

Ó Sé (*Gaelic* Oh'Shay) Translates to grandson or descendant of Sé

Siofra: (*noun Gaelic* Shee'fruh) Elf

Sumaire: (*noun Gaelic* Shoe MAH'ree) Vampire

Don't miss out!

Visit the website below and you can sign up to receive emails whenever Anna Rose publishes a new book. There's no charge and no obligation.

https://books2read.com/r/B-A-MFMF-CAUS

BOOKS 2 READ

Connecting independent readers to independent writers.

About the Author

Anna Rose is the author of the Tales of the Dragonguard (about dragons, of course!) and The Sumaire Web series of vampire novels.

She is currently working on KAL'S HEART, the third story in the Tales of the Dragonguard, that began with AYA'S DRAGON, and continues with SARA'S FIRE. which is now available in both e-book and softcover at Amazon, and in ebook format at iTunes, Barnes & Noble, and other fine merchants.

KAL'S HEART continues the story of the high-flying Dragonguard. Kal, the Aerie-born son of Dragonguard parents, is faced with a mystery that affects not only the whole of the Dragonguard, but his family as well. Together, he and his unusual dragon, Spirit, must use their unique abilities to find out who is causing trouble for the Dragonguard and to his family.

Her newest venture with her stories and novels is turning them into audiobooks for those folks who prefer listening to books, rather than reading them, for whatever reason.

Amongst her other writing, Anna writes vampires who like what they are and aren't looking for a rescue. Her vampires bite, drink and kill. No bottled or bagged blood for these vampires!

The first novel in the series, SIOFRA, was released in late January of 2012. The first novel was followed by FIACH FOLA and then DROCH FOLA. There is also a short story called FEASTA FOLA. Anna is also working on the fourth novel in the Sumaire Web series, COSAN FOLA, which she hopes to have completed by the end of 2018.

She lives in usually sunny Southern California.

Read more at www.sumaire.com.